THE BOTHY

TREVOR MARK THOMAS was born in Manchester in 1976. He lives with his girlfriend. He has a dog called Columbo.

THE BOTHY

TREVOR MARK THOMAS

CROMER

PUBLISHED BY SALT PUBLISHING 2019

2 4 6 8 10 9 7 5 3 1

Copyright © Trevor Mark Thomas 2019

First published in Great Britain in 2019 by
Salt Publishing Ltd
12 Norwich Road, Cromer NR27 0AX United Kingdom

www.saltpublishing.com

Salt Publishing Limited Reg. No. 5293401

A CIP catalogue record for this book is available from the British Library

ISBN 978 1 78463 160 4 (Paperback edition)
ISBN 978 1 78463 161 1 (Electronic edition)

Typeset in Neacademia by Salt Publishing

Printed and bound in Great Britain by Clays Ltd, Elcograf S.p.A

To my Mum and Dad

THE BOTHY

CHAPTER ONE

S OMEONE HAD WARNED Tom to stay away from Stephanie's funeral. Bricks had been thrown through his window, threats daubed on his front door. He sat on the edge of his bed looking at a picture of her. It had been taken the year before on a fine spring morning. They had gone up the Galata Tower. Stephanie was smiling, with the vast city rolling out behind her towards the Bosphorus. On the back of the photo she had drawn a heart in blue biro.

There was a knock at the door. Gary came into the room. He scratched at his beard and looked at the four paintings on the wall. He touched the cracked framing glass and asked, 'Are these hers?'

'Yeah,' said Tom.

Gary looked closely at one of the paintings. 'Is that a bird?'

'They're all birds.'

Gary stepped back and squinted. 'Was she any good?'

'What do you think?'

'I can't tell with this modern stuff.'

Tom put the photo of Stephanie back in his wallet. He lay down and put his head on the pillow. He could still smell her hair. Apricots and perspiration.

'We need to leave,' said Gary. 'They might be here soon.'

'I know.'

'We go now we can miss the traffic from Sheffield.'

Tom took his watch from the bedside table and

fastened the plastic strap. 'Are you sure he'll be able to help?'

'He's a good guy. Lives in the middle of nowhere. In an old pub. No-one goes there. It'll be quiet.'

'What does he get out of it?'

'I told him you're a good worker. How you can pull a good pint. Decent man to have around. He'll keep you nice and busy. It'll give me time to talk with Stephanie's parents. Make sure common sense prevails.'

'They won't see sense.'

'They will. In time.'

'How long?'

'They'll cool down eventually.'

'Two months?'

'Tops.' Gary patted Tom's knee. 'Get packed. We'll be up there by the time it gets dark.'

Tom got off the bed and packed underpants and socks. A few T-shirts. Some jeans. Thick jumpers. He put on his shoes and coat.

'That everything?'

Tom nodded, lifted up the rucksack on to his shoulder, and followed Gary out of the house. Before he closed the door, he looked back at his lounge, his kitchen.

They walked out on to the street. Litter in the gutters. Distant police sirens. Gary's white car was parked on a single yellow line. The windscreen was streaked with grime and the front licence plate was secured with tape. One of the wing mirrors had been snapped off.

Tom saw an old lady walking a terrier that wore a red knitted coat. The wool was wet and splashed with mud. Gary smiled at the dog and the old lady tugged down at the purple beret on her head.

'It's supposed to snow,' she said.

'Too warm for that,' replied Gary.

'Off out somewhere nice?'

Gary nodded. 'Camping.'

She looked up at the sky and frowned. Her dog barked at a crisp packet and started to bite the lead. She scolded it and walked on down the street.

Gary drove them away from the house. Narrow, dirty roads. Streets lined with boarded-up shops and thriving tanning salons, their needle-tipped neon signs shimmering in the rain. They passed by garages and depots fenced off by metal pickets looped with rusting barbed wire. Further on, there were locksmiths and bookies, pound shops and take-aways. Pubs with frosted windows. The pavements covered with cigarette butts and blackened ovals of gum. Smashed up bus shelters and rows of steel-shuttered shops. Towering above the grey streets, old mills and factories appeared black against the sky and small red lights flashed on the top of brick chimneys and yellow metal cranes.

Tom saw a school surrounded by chainlink fences. Prefab classrooms and empty playgrounds. Netball courts marked out with dirty white paint. A solitary child walking across muddy playing fields. Further out from the city, they drove past a business park. The glass and steel offices were separated by wide avenues and faded green lawns. A broken fountain was wrapped in hazard tape.

They were held up by a bad accident on a slip road. Two overturned cars. Dazed commuters milled about on the hard shoulder and watched a team of paramedics attempting to resuscitate a man in a torn grey suit.

A light rain drummed on the roof of the car. Tom wiped

away the condensation from the window and looked out as they left the grey city behind. Soon, they reached the hills and the roads narrowed. They passed by signs warning of the number of incidents. The number of deaths.

The red sun dipped below the hills and distant quarries were covered by a veil of blue shadow. A couple of stray sheep ate grass on the side of the road. Tom saw a sign welcoming them to Lancashire.

'Pagan country now,' said Gary, smiling. 'Story I heard is when Frank first moved up here, he actually had his men move that sign a couple of miles up the road so he could say his pub was in Yorkshire.'

Tom looked over at the valleys and cloughs covered with gorse and heather. The concealed and vibrant life of upland flushes. Woods of pine and birch. Gritstone ridges ran through the peat moorlands and acres of brown heather. The outline of rocks resembled bad teeth and jutting bones. The weather cleared. Clouds parted and a pale moon hung low in the sky. Ahead, the hills were fringed with the orange glow of sodium lights. The source of the light was a single building by the roadside that sat between two hills.

Gary nodded at it. 'There it is. The Bothy.'

'Let's turn back.'

'Tom. You can't go back. It's too dangerous.'

'They're right to want me dead, aren't they?'

'Tom—'

'I did it. Didn't I? I killed her.'

Gary stopped the car on a grass verge a couple of hundred metres away from the Bothy. He turned off the engine and tapped the steering wheel with his fingers. Tom wiped tears from his eyes.

4

'It's okay, mate,' said Gary. 'None of this is easy. But you have to stop thinking like this.'

'I can't.'

'You must. Listen: no-one will come looking for you up here. Up here belongs to Frank. This is his fucking world.'

Tom looked at the Bothy and dried his eyes with the heel of his hand.

'Do you trust him?' asked Tom.

'Tough but fair,' nodded Gary. 'That's what we always used to say about him.'

'You spoke to him though? The other day?'

'Nice to hear the old bastard's voice again. It's been a while.'

'I'm not sure about this, Gary.'

'You've got no choice,' said Gary. 'Listen: you keep quiet about what happened with Stephanie. Okay?'

'What do I say?'

'Make something up. Tell them you're in trouble with the police.'

'The police?'

'He'll always side against the law. And I know he's helped out other people in the past. Most of them on the run. Some desperate. But he helps them. Do right by him and I know he'll do right by you.'

'Is he dangerous?'

'Just do as you're told and you'll be okay,' said Gary. 'Here. Did you bring any gloves with you?'

'No.'

Gary reached into his pockets and handed him a pair of suede gloves. They both got out of the car and stood for a moment in the cold. Tom gazed upwards at a sky frosted with stars and hitched up his rucksack. He put on the gloves.

'Anything changes, I'll call Frank,' said Gary. 'I'll call you.'

'Okay.'

'And send my regards to Mandy.'

'Who's that?'

'Frank's wife. You'll like her.'

Gary got back in the car, tooted his horn, and drove away.

The Bothy was large and squat. A chimney coughed out thick, rubber-smelling smoke. The site was surrounded by stone walls, rough picket fences, and sheets of corrugated iron seven feet high. A red pickup truck was parked around the side of the building. He could smell sewage.

An old Christmas tree lay on its side near the front entrance to the pub. Tom looked up at the sign above the door. Gold lettering flaked away from the wooden board. He entered the bar through a small lobby. There was a smell of peat and damp. The low ceiling was supported by black-painted beams, each decorated with horse brasses. A specials board hung on the far wall and it was covered in profanities written with blue and green chalk.

Near the front window, two men sat on a long wooden bench varnished the colour of treacle. The men sipped at their beers, watching him carefully as he approached the bar. One of the men had jaundiced skin. His eyes were slightly crossed, as if he'd been hit over the head a few too many times. The other man wore a blue anorak. A piece of gauze plugged his right ear.

A short man with a cold sore on his bottom lip stood behind the bar reading a newspaper. He wore an apron that was a little small for him. He had tucked the frayed strings into his pockets

Three beer pumps were loosely bolted to the counter. A

collection box for mountain rescue sat on the counter. There was a rickety shelf stocked with spirits. Next to it, a cork board was covered in faded postcards and rested against the back wall.

'What do you want?' asked the barman.

Tom put his rucksack down and took off his gloves. 'Are you Frank?'

'Who the fuck are you?'

'Tom. Tom Staten.'

'Don't know the name.'

'Gary told you.'

'Don't know the name.'

'It's about a job,' said Tom.

'No jobs up here, mate.'

'I was told to speak to Frank.'

The barman washed his hands in the sink at the back. He dried his hands on a tea towel.

'Is Frank here?'

'If you want to speak with him,' said the barman over his shoulder, 'you'll have to wait.'

'Will he be long?'

'Yes, he will be fucking long.'

The two men in the corner smirked and sipped their drinks.

'Buy a drink or something,' he said.

Tom rubbed his forehead. 'Right. I'll have – I'll have beer then. What do you have?'

'Bitter. Pilsner. Heavy.'

'Heavy?'

'Porter,' said the barman.

'A bitter, please.'

'Bitter's off.'

'Pilsner?'

'Fuck off with that.' He poured a pint of porter and took Tom's ten pound note and put it in the old cash register. Tom was not given any change.

'Is there a bathroom?' asked Tom.

'You taking a shit?'

'No.'

'Back there.'

The barman pointed towards the fireplace. Beyond it, there was a metal door. It was chained shut. Tom walked past a pool table. A cue lay on the torn red baize. The cue ball was marked with flecks of blue chalk. He reached another door which led through to a bathroom. Its floor was covered with tattered off-white linoleum patterned with fern leaves. There was a stainless steel urinal. Just above it, a framed black-and-white photograph hung from the wall. It was a naked woman from the 1920s. She wore pearls and had a Louise Brooks haircut. He had a piss and then washed his hands with a cracked disc of soap.

Tom returned to his seat and sipped his porter. It caught the back of his throat. He looked outside, through the bullseye glass. The Christmas tree had moved. It had been blown about by the wind. He took out his mobile phone and checked it. There was no signal. He heard a noise from the floor above. A slammed door. A creaking floorboard.

The man with gauze in his ear rose out of his seat and walked towards Tom. The blue anorak strained over his gut. Tom caught the bad smell of tobacco and unwashed clothes.

'What's your name, mate?'

'Tom.'

8

'You buying me a drink, Tom?' asked the man. 'You should buy me a drink. Ken? Tucker? Tom's buying.'

Ken – the barman – shook his head and went back to cleaning glasses.

'Ask him if he's got any ciggies, Braudy,' said Tucker, scratching his chin with fingernails stained with nicotine. He stared at him with his crossed eyes.

'Bring any cigarettes with you?'

'No,' replied Tom.

Braudy unzipped his anorak and hung it over the back of a chair. Tom pulled out another ten pound note from his wallet. The photograph of Stephanie slipped out. Braudy picked it up and smiled.

'Who's this?'

Tom snatched back the photo. 'No-one,' he said.

'Who was it?' asked Tucker.

'A girl.'

'She your bit of stuff?'

Tom put the photo back into his wallet and handed over the money. No change was given. Braudy got his pint and sat opposite Tom. He turned his good ear towards him, and asked, 'You come far?'

'Leeds.'

'Thought you were a Manc.'

'You guys come drinking here often?'

Braudy laughed. 'No cunt comes drinking up here.'

There was shouting from upstairs. Braudy picked up one of the suede gloves. 'These yours?'

'A mate's.'

He touched the material. 'Nice. Expensive?'

'You'd have to ask my mate.'

The noise above stopped. Braudy gazed at the ceiling and said, 'So you're here to work?'

'Yeah.'

'If you needed work you could find it in Leeds. Plenty of jobs there.'

'I wanted to come here.'

'No-one wants to come here,' he said. 'What's the real reason?'

Upstairs, there were slammed doors. Then silence. Braudy adjusted the gauze and gulped back his drink.

Tom sighed. 'There's been – there's been trouble.'

'What kind of trouble?'

'Police, mostly.'

'Police mostly. What else?'

'How do you mean?'

'If you're in trouble with police mostly, you're in trouble with something else too.'

'I'd rather talk about this with Frank.'

'You work up here, you'll be taking bread out of our fucking mouths. So tell us.'

Tom looked down at his pint and shook his head gently. Braudy glared at him and picked up his drink and his anorak. He put the glass on the bar. He signalled to Tucker and the two of them left through a wooden door. Tom took another mouthful of beer and swallowed it back. It was starting to taste better.

Ken carefully polished a set of shot glasses. The wooden door squeaked open. A figure stood there in shadow. The door closed again and Ken put his cloth on one of the beer pumps.

'You're up,' he said. 'Leave your rucksack here. Go through to the office.'

Tom got up and pushed through the wooden door. He entered a murky room. It looked more like a workshop than an office. There was a heavy smell of sweat and alcohol. A green angle-poise lamp sat on a filing cabinet and illuminated scores of out-of-date calendars hanging on the walls. Some of them were dated from the early 1980s. They all featured naked women posing on beaches. Big hair. On their knees. Glossy and unconvincing smiles. The floor was laid with fuzzy carpet tiles. Some were stained with damp, others had gone mouldy. A circular saw sat on a wooden workbench and three electric drills were laid out on a desk. In the corner, several board games sat on a shelf. A steel-plated cribbage board and a number of colourful pegs stored in a small plastic bag. Two battered packs of cards, a Spirograph, a Mahjong set, and a copy of a game called Pit. Beneath the shelf, a box of old magazines sat on top of a VHS machine.

A middle-aged man sat at a plastic table. He had a bottle of whisky in front of him and held a bag of frozen peas over his right eye. His nose was bulbous and mottled. He wore brown corduroy trousers held up by braces the colour of fresh lemons. His white shirt was open at the neck, the sleeves rolled up.

'I'm Tom.'

'I know who you are.' Frank took the frozen peas away and blinked. The skin around his eye was red. He opened the bottle of whisky. 'Glasses in the sideboard behind you.'

'Nothing for me.'

'Glass, then.'

Tom handed him a glass, and watched him pour a double for himself. The face of Frank's chunky gold watch was scratched and the second hand was jammed halfway round. Frank knocked back the whisky and lit a cigarette with a gold

Dupont lighter. He stared at Tom for a few moments. He was unsmiling. Deep in thought. 'So Gary sent you,' he said. 'Not seen him for years. You work for him?'

'At his snooker hall. He sends his regards. To you and – Mandy, is it?'

Frank blew out a plume of smoke and said, 'We don't see too much of Mandy these days.'

'Oh. No. Sorry.'

'She left under a bit of a cloud.'

'I didn't think. I heard—'

'Arguing? That was Cora.' He sniffed and pushed the glass into the middle of the table. 'Why are you here, Tom?'

'Did Gary say anything?'

'I want to hear it from you.'

'Gary told me to keep quiet.'

'We can keep it between ourselves. But I need to know,' he said. 'So. Come on. Out with it.'

'My girlfriend died.' He paused. 'It was a car accident.'

'So?'

'Her family don't believe in accidents.'

'Catholic?'

'They just want me dead.'

Frank pushed at the bag of frozen peas and asked, 'Would I know who they are? The family?'

'They're involved in all sorts. Whatever makes them money.'

'Surname?'

'Conway.'

'Yeah. I know him. Big house near Preston. Likes his women young, doesn't he?' Frank picked at his teeth. 'Clever man. Not to be tangled with.'

'He's put out a contract on me,' said Tom.

'How much?'

'Don't know. But want to keep the thing quiet if I can. Just in case. This kind of news can carry.'

Frank thought for a moment. 'Here's what we'll do. I'll tell the boys you've been caught stealing some money.'

'I've done nothing wrong.'

'You feel guilty though?'

'I try to think what I could have done differently.'

'Aye. That's called guilt. Best get used to that feeling, Tom. It won't go away,' said Frank, looking into his glass. 'Besides, the boys won't believe you've done nothing wrong. Better to tell stories sometimes.'

'I don't want to cause trouble.'

'You got caught stealing. Right?' He clicked his fingers, searching for the words. 'Because you needed money for your mum's operation.'

'I don't have a mum.'

'Her funeral, then.' Frank put his glass down and straightened his shirt. He lifted the braces back on to his shoulders. 'Come with me.'

Tom followed Frank from the small room, and back into the warmth of the bar. Frank picked up the cue lying on the pool table. He looked down the shaft to see if it was true or not. He pulled a face and hung the cue on the brass rack screwed to the wall.

'Need some money,' said Frank.

'Notes?'

'Nah.'

Ken opened the cash register and handed Frank a plastic bag of pound coins.

'Take Tom out to the caravan. Make sure he has what he needs.'

Tom picked up his rucksack.

'That's a small bag,' said Ken.

'Didn't think I'd be staying for long.'

Ken took off his apron, and threw it over the bar. He did up the top button of his shirt and put on a dirty green Puffa jacket. Tom followed Ken out to the small hallway where the bathroom was. There was a white cupboard in the corner. Ken opened it and handed Tom bedding and a red towel.

'There are more blankets here if you need them.'

'Okay if I have one more?'

'Help yourself.'

Tom took out a tartan blanket and folded it up. Ken unchained the back door and stepped out into the yard. A security light clicked on. There were two caravans. One was practically in ruins. The other was not and looked like a newer model. Amongst the skips there were piles of bricks, cans of creosote. Bags of hardened cement.

Ken led Tom towards the newer caravan. Its wheels were up on bricks. He opened the door, stepped inside, and switched on the light. Tom climbed in after him and ducked beneath the ceiling. Beige curtains covered the windows, and the walls were decorated with wood chip painted the shade of mustard powder. There was a kitchen area. A kettle, a refrigerator. A jar of hot chocolate, a couple of mugs. Some dead flies, a box of pink condoms.

At the back of the caravan, a fold-out dining table was held in place with a length of bungee cord. At the front, a sweat-stained mattress lay on the Formica floor. A crack in the window was covered with duct tape and cardboard.

'There's a heater,' said Ken. 'Put it on now and you won't wake up with ice in your hair.'

'Okay.'

Ken opened the fridge. There was an old packet of salt beef and squares of processed cheese slices. He picked up an open carton of milk and sniffed it. 'Might be on the turn. Give it a huff before you try it. Been there for a while. Other than that, everything's catered for.'

'When do you need me tomorrow?' asked Tom.

'Make it before ten,' said Ken, walking towards the door. 'Oh, and when the weather's like this, always wear two pairs of underpants. And a hat. A deerstalker. Frank told me some cunt lost their ears from the cold.'

'I don't have a hat.'

'Find one then.'

Ken left the caravan. He walked back into the main building, blowing into his cupped hands. The security light clicked off. Tom closed the door and put down his rucksack. The bedding was old. The duvet was dark blue. Moth-eaten. The pillows were marked with brown sweat stains. He made himself some hot chocolate and switched on the heater. The three bars turned from grey, to yellow, to cherry. Slowly, the caravan was infused with heat and the smell of dust.

CHAPTER TWO

TOM AWOKE TO the sound of rain pattering on the roof of the caravan. A draught blew in through the crack in the window. He checked his watch. It was nine. He reached over to the electric heater and flicked it on. As it warmed up, he tried to think of other things. Work. Routine. The day ahead. He licked his dry lips. His breath smelled bad. He got out of bed and wondered if he should wear two pairs of underpants, unsure whether or not Ken was joking. He dressed in jeans and a jumper. Plenty of layers would do the trick.

In the bar, there was a smell of fresh coffee and stale tobacco. Embers in the fireplace glowed red. Standing on the hearth was an ornate brass fireguard shaped like a fan. Frank was behind the bar. He was writing in a thick ledger with a blue fountain pen. Ken was sitting at a table, reading an old issue of *National Geographic*.

Sitting on the counter was an old coffee machine. The carafe was full. There was an open can of condensed milk and a few mugs and tea spoons. Tom looked at the cork board filled with faded postcards from around the world. A few were sent from Spanish resorts and featured women posing in bikinis. A couple had been sent from Corsica.

Frank's bruise from the night before had come out as a faint blue mark beneath his right eye. He was wearing an old polo shirt. It was faded orange and the neck was pulled out of shape. His canvas trousers were black and there was brick dust on the knees and thighs. He had a full ashtray in front of him. A drop of ink fell from the nib of the pen and splashed on one of the pages. He tore out the blotted page, screwed it up, and threw it in the fire. He lit a cigarette and said to Ken, 'Get Tom a coffee.'

Ken nodded and folded the page he was reading. Tom could see his clothes were creased. There was a smell of sour milk. Ken poured coffee into a red mug. He stirred in some condensed milk and added a few spoonfuls of white sugar. Then he filled a fresh cup and pushed it towards Tom.

'Milk is there if you want it,' he said.

Tom sipped the coffee. It tasted strange. He noticed an old television in the corner. A makeshift aerial had been fashioned from a coat hanger, stretched out into a vague diamond shape. Near the front door, there was a wooden shelf of small sporting trophies. Three of the trophies were for golf. One was for darts. The golf trophies had a faux marble plinth and were topped with tiny figures made from silver-coloured plastic. One of the figures had lost its head. The darts trophy consisted of a single metal dart. The red plastic flight was chipped.

Frank went back to his ledger and added a few numbers into a column. The handwriting was flowing and exact. He did not look up, and said, 'Ken will take you around the grounds. He can give you a few jobs to do.'

Tom finished his drink and Ken put on a black wool coat. He did up the shiny buttons, picked out a blue cagoule from the lobby, and handed it to Tom. The cagoule was too big. He left it unzipped and they went outside. It was still raining. The wind was cold. Ken walked over to the red pickup truck. Rust flecked the bodywork and the radiator grilles were bent and twisted. A filthy teddy bear had been tied to the bumper with metal wire. Its eyes had fallen off and it had no mouth. Ken patted the bonnet.

'Any good with cars?' he asked.

'Not really.'

Ken shook his head. 'This one has a hundred thousand miles on the clock. Still runs okay.'

'Had it long?'

'Five years,' he said, kicking at the tires. 'I service it. Keep it ticking over. Never failed an MOT yet. Can you drive?'

'Yeah.'

Tom noticed the Christmas tree he had seen the night before. Its branches were snagged on the barbed wire fence.

'Go and pick up that tree,' said Ken, hawking up some phlegm.

Tom dragged the tree away from the fence, leaving a trail of brown pine needles in his wake. He looked back at the building. A few windows were boarded up. Black paint peeled from the window frames and the eaves. The roof was covered in moss and the gutters were choked with dead leaves and the failed nests of birds.

'You still get customers coming up here?' asked Tom.

'Lost hikers, mostly. They don't stay long.'

'Shame. It could be a nice spot.'

'His wife had run a couple of pubs before.'

'Mandy?'

He shielded his eyes from the sun. 'How do you know about her?'

'My mate Gary told me.'

'And how did he know her?'

'I don't know.'

'Wouldn't say her name to Frank if I were you.'

They wandered over to a large metal shed. The corrugated iron roof had pieces of steel bolted on to conceal the holes. Ken unlocked the wooden door and Tom saw shelves of tools lining the walls. Screws and nails, all sorted into boxes according to type and size. A row of orange-handled screwdrivers hung from a steel pegboard. Propped up against the wall there were offcuts of wood and plasterboard and an outboard motor. The starter cord was wrapped around the propeller. Ken moved a barbecue out of the way. He lifted up a bag of old paint brushes. They were still wet with white paint. He put the bag aside and put two cartons of oil on the work surface.

'Frank said you've had a bit of trouble with police.'

'A little bit, yeah.'

'He said something about your mum being sick.'

Tom paused for a moment, trying to remember the lie Frank had wanted him to tell. Was it about his sick mother or his dead mother?

'Law never fucking care about things like that,' said Ken. 'Sick parents. Sick children. Makes no difference to them.'

He locked the door. Tom followed him around to the side of the shed. There was a chopping block on the ground. It was a thick chunk of wood bound by a car tyre. A large stack of cut logs were covered by tarpaulin. Tom added the tree to the wood pile and brushed the brown needles from his hands.

Ken reached under the tarp and brought out an axe. The blade was very sharp. He reached over and picked up the Christmas tree. 'You chop off the branches. Use it as kindling. Then you cut the trunk into foot-long sections. No more, no less. Same with any kind of wood. It burns more efficiently that way.'

'Foot-long sections. Okay.'

'Make sure you get it right,' said Ken, putting the axe back on the pile. He replaced the tarp. 'Frank is a real stickler for this kind of thing.'

At the back of the yard Tom saw a small fishing boat sitting on a steel trailer. The bow rails were nearly black with dirt and the stern was covered with faded green canvas. There were holes in the fibreglass hull and birds had nested in the cockpit. The name of the boat had been scratched off.

'We used to take this out to the coast,' he said. 'Like fishing, Tom?'

'Tried it a couple of times. On the canal.'

'Carp?'

'Pike.'

'Fishing's better at sea. More fun.'

Ken stopped by the caravan Tom had slept in. He ran his finger across the side of the caravan, leaving a white mark in the dirt. He bent down, picked up a crushed tin can, and tossed it in a skip. Nearby, there were a few wheelie bins. Numbers had been daubed on the sides in white paint. 802. 401. 123. Bottles poked out from the grey lids. Ken opened a bin and picked out a brown bottle.

'Good one, this. IPA. From Manchester.' He dropped the bottle back in the bin and walked on past the other caravan. Part of the roof had perished and filthy curtains hung out of the cracked windows. A battered door hung from rusting hinges. The interior walls were slimy with algae and something had built a nest in the kitchen sink.

Tom saw a tall metal frame sticking out of a concrete foundation. A loose strip of hazard tape was attached to one of the struts. Here and there, plastic sheeting poked through the cracks. Ken went over and kicked at the frame. He bent down and ran his fingers over the concrete. The surface crumbled away in his fingers. He tutted. 'Braudy put too much fucking sand in the mix.'

'What is it?'

'Climbing frame and swings. We were going to build a little playground and beer garden. Get more families up here. That's where the money is.'

A small animal had walked beneath the metal structure while the concrete had still been wet. Its tracks were still visible. Ken scuffed his feet on the ground. 'Septic tank under here too. Four thousand litres of shit. When full.'

'Is it?'

'Need to get it drained in a couple of months.' Ken strolled past a plastic bathtub lying on its side. Long strands of dirty hair hung from the plughole. He walked up to some gas canisters and a large green oil tank. Puddles of brown water glistened with bands of colour.

'Ever sounded a tank before?' asked Ken.

'Sound?'

Ken went over to the tank. 'You see this valve here? Unscrew it. Put a tape measure in there, and push it down until it hits the bottom. Then take the tape out, and see where the oil comes up to. Should be twenty-two inches. Thereabouts. Take a reading every couple of days.'

They walked alongside a high iron fence, shoes crunching on pieces of broken glass. Ken stopped by a hatch mounted in the side of the building. He took out a bunch of keys and unlocked the two padlocks. He lifted the hatch and went down some wooden steps. A light came on. Tom followed him. He saw nine beer barrels. Lines were neatly plumbed into three of the barrels. A few shelves held jars of eggs, bottles of bleach and boxes of soap powder. A roll of plastic sheeting leaned against the wall and, next to it, a single grey mattress had been pushed into the corner. Spots of mould grew on the damask covering.

Tom saw a few cardboard boxes which were filled with photo albums. Tom opened one up. He saw a picture of a dark-haired woman on the beach. She was middle-aged and looking over her shoulder towards the camera. Laughing. Her breasts were pressed against the soft white sand.

'Are these photos safe down here?' asked Tom.

'Safe from what?'

'Water.'

'Not my photos. Not my problem,' said Ken, walking over to a large metal cabinet. He checked the four padlocks and gave the door a rattle. He turned to Tom and pointed to one of the shelves.

'Pick up one of them jars of pickled eggs,' he said.

'Any particular one?'

'They're all the same.'

Tom reached up and carefully lifted one of the jars. It was heavy and covered in dust. When he moved it, a spider scurried out, and disappeared behind a box of screws. Ken climbed back up to the yard. Tom followed him, careful not to trip and drop the jar. Ken locked the hatch and they returned indoors.

Tucker and Braudy were sitting in the corner of the room. They were both playing cards. Tucker's yellow skin was paler in the sunlight. He held a hand over one of his eyes, deep in thought. Braudy sat back in his chair, smiling. They were playing with an old *Star Trek* deck. The corners of the cards were dog-eared.

Tom put the jar down on the counter. He wiped dust from his hands.

Ken opened a drawer behind the bar and handed Tom a small hardback note book. On the front of it, someone had written 'OIL'. A stubby pencil was tucked inside.

'Use this for the soundings,' said Ken. 'You write the date, and the measurement. If it gets below 10 inches, you tell me or Frank. Clear?'

'Yeah.'

Ken picked up a jar of Swarfega and washed the grime from his hands. Frank walked into the room. He held three sealed envelopes in his hands. Tom could hear the faint jingle of coins. He watched Frank go over to Tucker and Braudy. They both looked up from their game. Tucker threw down his cards and lit a cigarette with his plastic lighter.

Frank handed out the envelopes to Tucker, Braudy, and Ken. They tore open their envelopes. Money fell out. Notes, a few coins. Tucker quickly counted his, but slowed halfway through. He started again. His lips moving.

Ken folded up the money and put it in his top pocket.

Tucker stared at the money. 'This is a month's pay,' he said.

'So?'

'We're owed two.' Tucker shook his head. 'I was hoping to buy a few things.'

'A month will see you right for now,' said Frank. 'Not like you're running up debts, is it?'

'That's not the point.'

'You short of fucking food? Not able to pay the rent? School fees? Fucking missus nagging you for a new pair of fucking shoes?'

'Is him over there going to get paid too?' asked Tucker.

'We haven't discussed remuneration yet. Have we Tom? Anyway. You don't hear Ken or Braudy complaining,' said Frank.

'You know me, Frank. Grateful for the money.'

Braudy said nothing, gathered up his pay, and put it back in the envelope.

'Pint, Braudy?' asked Frank.

Braudy looked at his watch. 'Pay day pint. Yeah.'

Frank pulled up a stool, and sat down. 'Drink, Tom?'

'Bit early for me.'

'Tucker,' said Frank. 'Beer?'

Tucker stared out the window.

Frank put his feet on the brass foot rail and tore off the corners of a beer mat. 'The good news is I'm finding us new business. Something with Wayne.'

Tucker sneered and said, 'What? Another shitty knocking shop in Leeds?'

Frank took a long sip of his beer. 'You want to say that again?'

'Come on. Leave it, Frank,' said Ken.

'I want to hear him say that again,' said Frank.

Tucker coughed, played with his lighter, and looked away. He muttered something under his breath.

'Louder, Tucker. So we can hear you.'

'Doesn't matter.'

There was silence. Frank walked over to Tucker and lifted him by the collar. He held him close and whispered something in his ear. Tucker sat down again.

'Get the man a fucking beer,' said Frank.

CHAPTER THREE

T OM SIPPED AT a cup of hot chocolate and looked out
at the fog. He was wrapped in the tartan rug. The electric fire cast soft orange light across the Formica. A draught
stirred the dirty net curtains and birds hopped across the
roof, twittering brightly despite the murk of the morning. He
looked at the photograph of Stephanie and tried to remember
the day they had spent together. The sunlight and the warmth.
Walking hand in hand through busy streets.

He boiled the kettle again and poured the hot water into
the sink. He added some cold water and washed himself. After
dressing, he put on his coat and gloves. He slipped the photo
of Stephanie back into his wallet and put it in his pocket. It
was damp outside. He crossed the yard and left the grounds of
the Bothy through the front gate. He followed the wall around
until he could see the climbing frame and the oil tank. Wind
had blown rubbish into the steel pickets of the fence. Slimy
polythene bags, nibbled cartons, twisted tin cans. He moved
away from the fence and strolled through the long grass until
he found a path which led up to the top of the hill. A patch of
pine trees appeared as ghostly black shapes. The road below
vanishing into the grey fog.

He took out his mobile phone and held it up to see if he
could get a signal. Still nothing. He returned to the Bothy and
hung up his coat in the lobby. There was a smell of methylated
spirits and fried food. Four bains-marie were lined up on the

counter and each one was heated by a pale blue flame. A fresh batch of coffee was nearly brewed. Steam rose from the glass carafe.

Braudy and Tucker sat in the corner eating plates of fried food. Tucker wore an eyepatch. He cut a sausage into segments and ate each one noisily. Braudy put down his fork and wiped his hands on his scruffy red gilet. He looked at his watch and said, 'Three minutes late.'

'I went for a walk,' said Tom.

'Fire's getting low,' said Tucker.

'Did you cut any logs?'

'I forgot,' said Tom.

Tucker shook his head and finished his sausages.

Braudy took his plate over to the bar. He lifted the lid of a bain-marie. Inside, four sausages sat in pools of dark grease. They smelled delicious. Tom got himself a coffee and had it black. The door to the office opened and Ken emerged holding a plate full of fatty bacon. The cold sore on his lip had got worse. He scraped the bacon into a bain-marie and turned up the burners.

'You dressed for working outside?' asked Braudy.

'Yeah,' said Tom.

'Two pairs of underpants?'

'I thought that was a joke.'

'Not up here it isn't,' said Braudy. 'What about a hat?'

'Don't have one.'

Braudy squeezed brown sauce over his eggs. He put the sachet aside.

'Don't know how you can stand that stuff,' said Tucker.

'Offsets the saltiness.'

'Saltiness. Bollocks.' He went over to the counter and

26

looked inside a bain-marie. 'You fucked up your eggs, Ken.'

'They're cooked.'

'Yolks're hard. No-one likes hard yolks.'

'Frank does,' said Ken.

'Bollocks.' Tucker rubbed at his teeth with a red handkerchief. 'What's the new boy think? You like hard yolks?'

'They're okay.'

'Jesus.' Tucker took out a cigarette and lit it. He tapped his lighter on the table and stared at Tom.

After a while, Tom said, 'What is it we're doing today?'

'Bit of digging,' said Braudy. 'A few holes.'

'For drainage,' said Tucker.

Braudy chewed on his bacon and licked the grease off his fingers. 'Four holes in all.'

Tucker shook his head. 'Nah. Three.'

'Frank told me it was four.'

'It was three.'

Braudy stood up and finished his coffee. He stretched and checked his watch. 'We'll go in an hour.'

Tom went to the counter and picked up a fresh plate. He helped himself to bacon, eggs, black pudding, and sat down at an empty table. Tucker lifted his eyepatch. He blew at the tip of his cigarette and watched it glow orange. 'You not like eating with other people, Tom?'

'Didn't want to interrupt you smoking,' said Tom.

'Worried the smoke will mess with your fucking palate?'

Tom cut off some of the fat from the bacon.

'Hey. Princess. Talking to you.'

Tom put down his knife and fork. 'I just want to eat.'

Tucker smirked and replaced his eyepatch and went over to speak with Ken, who was behind the bar replacing one of the whisky optics. They covered their mouths as they spoke, casting sly glances at him as he sipped his coffee. After a few minutes, the two men left the room, leaving Tom on his own. He dipped the black pudding in the grease, closed his eyes and savoured the taste.

A door opened and he looked up. A girl walked into the room. She was short and wore an Ivy League hoodie and grey tracksuit bottoms. Her eyes were green and her hair was black and tied back. She carried a plate of grapefruit and a cup of tea. There was a magazine tucked under her left arm. She set down her breakfast and sat at the adjacent table. She flicked through the magazine, wafting the scent of perfume samples in his direction. She tore out an advert for a holiday. Somewhere faraway. Blue skies and dusty landscapes.

'Where's that?' asked Tom.

'Jordan.' She nodded towards the window. 'Off out in that today?'

'Digging holes.'

'You wrapped up for the cold? Two pairs of underpants and a hat?'

'Thought they were kidding.'

'Does seem like a load of bollocks, doesn't it?'

'Sorry – what's your name?'

'Cora,' she said. 'You?'

'Tom.'

They both looked out at the fog. It was getting thicker. Cora shivered.

'What's the coffee like this morning, Tom?'

'Weak. But not bad.'

She went back to her magazine and flicked through to the end. She put the magazine aside and started to eat the grapefruit with a teaspoon. Fine jets of juice squirted out on to the table.

Tom took out his mobile phone again. There was still no signal.

'Best off using the phone behind the bar,' said Cora.

Braudy walked in from the back. He was doing up his belt and zipping up his fly.

'Best off doing what, Cora?' he asked.

'Using the phone.'

'For what?'

'To call my friend,' said Tom. 'Gary.'

'You can call him now,' said Braudy. 'I won't listen.'

'I'll do it later.'

'Tom's here for a bit of manual labour. Brawn. Like a bit of muscle, don't you, Cora?'

She pushed her cup away and stood up. She walked off, leaving her breakfast behind. She moved one of the horse brasses hanging from a ceiling beam.

Braudy watched her leave. 'Proper bitch,' he said. 'Tucker fucking hates her.'

'You?'

'She's a daft cow. Look-but-don't-touch type, you know? Put some noses out of joint when she came up here last year. Just after Frank's wife moved out.'

'Where did she go?'

'Back to Liverpool.' He went over to the horse brass and pushed it so it was straight again. He put a coat on and went out the front door. The cold air from outside made the burners gutter and flare. Tom went to the phone behind the bar. Above the fridges, someone had covered a sheet of cardboard with foreign currency. Mostly coins. The phone was an old green

BT model and was mounted on the wall. Phone numbers had been scratched into. Names. A heart with an arrow through it.

He dialled Gary's number. The phone rang a few times before it was answered. There were coughs on the other end of the line.

'Gary? It's Tom.'

'Tom! How are you getting on?'

'Just had breakfast.'

There was a sneeze. 'How's Frank?'

'Not spoken much with him.'

'He'll warm up.'

Tom looked around the room. He picked up the charity box. One coin rattled in it. 'Have you heard anything? Stephanie's family? Anything like that?'

'They found out you skipped town,' said Gary. 'They trashed your place.'

'I thought they might.'

'I've boarded up the windows. Tried to make sure things are secure.'

'Thank you.'

'Not what you wanted to hear, I know. But this will take time.'

'Sure.'

'But you've done the right thing. Okay?'

'Sure.'

'Look after yourself.'

Tom hung up the phone. Outside, the fog had worsened. He could no longer see the hill across the road. The floorboards creaked above and he heard the voice of the girl. Cora. He wondered where Frank had met her. Why she had come up here. He listened to the voices for a while longer.

At about half-ten Braudy and Tucker entered the bar. Both men were laughing. Tucker sat on the pool table and rolled the cue ball across the baize. The ball rattled in the jaws of the top pocket. Ken came in holding a plastic bag containing flasks of coffee and sandwiches wrapped in silver foil. Tucker looked in the plastic bag.

'What have you made us?'

'Some tuna. Some chicken.'

'Any cheese?'

Ken nodded and took out the truck keys and accidentally dropped them on the floor. His knees cracked when he knelt down to pick them up. He handed them to Braudy.

'Don't fucking lose them,' said Ken.

'I know, I know,' said Braudy.

Tom fetched his coat and suede gloves from the lobby. He put them on and checked he had his wallet with him.

'You're not going to need money, pal.'

'Tom's keeping an eye on his valuables,' said Tucker, giving a sly smile.

'What about a hat?'

Tom shrugged and said, 'I don't have one.'

Braudy checked his coat. 'Shit. I've lost it. Tucker. Spare hat?'

Tucker put his hat on and patted the top of his head. 'Nope.'

'I'll be okay,' said Tom, quietly.

They stepped out into the cold and walked through the fog towards the store. It creaked in the wind. Braudy unlocked the door and took out three rusting shovels and handed them to Tom. Tucker picked up a toolbox and brought out four signposts about a metre high. Each one read: 'Butty Van. Hot food to go'.

'Can you drive, Tom?' asked Braudy.

'Sure.'

'Fog not too thick?'

'I'll manage.'

They loaded the red pickup truck and climbed in. A small sock monkey charm hung from the rearview mirror. Tom turned on the ignition. The steering wheel was sticky. So was the gear stick. Braudy switched on the heater and adjusted the setting. There was a blast of air and a smell of dust.

They sat for a few moments, waiting for the cabin to warm up. Tucker lit a limp roll up. It hung from his bottom lip. The smoke was foul-smelling. Acrid. Tom switched on the fog lights and put the truck into reverse. He eased it out on to the road.

They drove for a quarter of a mile and Braudy instructed him to take a right. Tom slowed down as they reached the top of a blind hill. Braudy looked over at the dashboard and said, 'Engine's running warm.'

'I'll take it easy.'

'Give it less on the gas,' said Tucker. 'Easy on the clutch too.'

'Bit of a lead foot, aren't you Tom?' laughed Braudy.

The truck climbed the hilly roads. The engine strained with the effort. In the wing mirror, Tom could see black exhaust fumes trailing behind the truck.

'Turn off the heater, Braudy.'

'Cold's no good for my ear,' replied Braudy.

'Stop being so bloody soft,' said Tucker. He turned off the heater and went back to rolling his cigarettes.

They soon reached a bigger road and drove along it for a couple of miles.

'Stop at this junction,' said Braudy.

Tom stopped the truck and Braudy jumped out. He took one of the 'Butty Van' signs and went over to a patch of long grass by the road. After hammering the sign into the soft ground, he got back in the truck.

'Take a left,' he said.

The road narrowed, and Tom slowed down, afraid of hitting the stone walls. The truck topped a rise and the road curved right before straightening out. There was a lay-by on the left.

'Just here,' said Braudy.

Tom parked the truck near a fence constructed from light-coloured wood. He turned off the engine. They all climbed out. Tom handed Braudy the keys to the truck and put on his suede gloves. He saw the teddy bear attached to the truck's front bumper.

'He got a name?' he asked.

'Thinking of calling him 'Tom',' said Tucker, flicking his roll-up on to the grass.

Braudy took two shovels from the flatbed of the truck and handed them to Tucker. He picked up the remaining signs and a club hammer.

'You two go on ahead. This won't take long,' said Braudy, walking back down the road.

Tom picked up the packed lunches and walked away with Tucker. They followed the road until they reached a dirt track. Tom could hear the dull rhythmic thud of hammering.

'Your ears cold yet?' asked Tucker, checking the blades on the shovels.

'They're okay. Bit raw,' said Tom. 'So what are those signs for?'

'Code, isn't it? So we can direct Wayne's lot to where we've dug the holes.'

'So why "Butty Van"?'

Tucker did not answer and climbed over a wall. He jumped down and slipped on the wet grass. Tom followed him. They joined a mud trail that meandered away towards a cluster of pine trees. There were shallow, silvery pools of standing water. There was a dead rabbit lying near a stone wall. Its eyes had been pecked out.

'Been talking with Braudy,' said Tucker. 'Telling him that we've probably been a bit hard on you.'

'It's nothing.'

'Know the saying though, don't you? Catch more with honey than vinegar. I remember what it was like when I first came up here. Like starting school or something.'

'I've been vouched for,' said Tom. 'The guy I worked for. Gary—'

'You keep saying "Gary" like he's a fucking celebrity.'

'A few people know who Gary is in Leeds.'

'Not in Leeds now, are you?'

'Okay, but Frank and his mates used to go to Gary's snooker hall.'

'When?'

'Ten, fifteen years ago?'

'Not exactly blood brothers, are they? And anyway it doesn't mean Frank knows *you*, does it?'

'I thought he was going to say something to you. Explain why I was here.'

'He did. Sounded like bullshit to me.'

The bottom of Tom's trouser legs were damp. His feet were cold. The path was getting muddier. He walked past a tussock of cottongrass. Spiked leaves glistened with moisture.

'Three years ago a fella came up here. Name was Favel,' said Tucker. 'Bit like you. Didn't tell me, or anyone else who he was. Frank – soft as shite when he wants to be – let it slide. Know what happened?'

Tom shook his head.

'This fella Favel fucked us over, didn't he? Took some things that weren't his. Went back to the city with what he'd stolen. Made a pretty penny. Now, to a guy like you, that sounds like nothing. Right?'

'I'm not here to steal money from you.'

'This isn't about fucking money. It's about trust, mate. Trust.'

'It's not like that.'

'It fucking is,' said Tucker. 'Which is why I'm asking you – nicely – to tell me why you're here. Just so I can at least know you're on the fucking level. Just so I can have at least one reason to like you. Because I'm guessing you're not a man in possession of a fucking marvellous singing voice.'

Tom looked at the ground, the thinning path. The plastic bag containing the lunches caught on the barbs of a gorse bush. The fog was getting thicker. He listened out for birdsong but could not hear anything other than their own footsteps on the grass. Tucker stabbed his shovel into the ground and pulled out a hat from his pocket. He dangled it in front of Tom. 'See, if I trusted you, you'd have toasty ears.'

Tom reached for the hat, but Tucker stuffed it back into his pocket.

'Tosser,' said Tom.

'Wrong: a tosser with warm ears.'

'Frank told me there was no hurry.'

'What Frank tells you, and what his men want, aren't always the same thing,' said Tucker. 'Tell me what you fucking did.'

Tom took off his gloves and scratched at his hands. 'It's the police,' he said. 'They want me.'

'The police want everybody. Try again.'

'That's all I have.'

Tucker pulled his shovel out of the ground. Considered the blade. 'You rape someone?'

'No. I didn't rape anyone,' said Tom.

'Did you rob someone? Murder them?'

'No.'

'Something to do with that bird of yours? One in the photo?'

'Leave it, Tucker.'

'Knock her up, did you?'

'Leave it.'

Tucker swung the shovel. Tom dodged out of the way but stumbled and fell on his back. He dropped the bag of lunches. Tucker knelt on Tom's shoulders and slapped him hard with the back of his hand. Tom struggled and Tucker hit him again.

'Tell me who you are.'

'It's the police.'

'Bollocks, police. What did you do?'

'It was an accident.'

'Liar.' Tucker slapped Tom again, and shouted, 'Let me see that fucking picture of her. One in your wallet.'

'No!'

'Worried I might recognise her, Tom?'

'Fuck off.'

Tucker flipped Tom on to his front and reached into his pockets, searching for the wallet. Tom felt finger tips brush his thighs and arse. His balls. He threw back a sharp elbow and caught Tucker on the cheek. He shouted and grabbed Tom by the hair. He pushed his face into the mud.

'What did you *do* to her, Tom?'

'Please—'

Tom heard whistling. He saw a silhouette in the fog and called out. The whistling stopped. Tom managed to break free and Tucker rolled away. They both lay on the ground like a pair of exhausted and disappointed lovers. Tucker took out one of his crooked roll-ups. He lit it and blew smoke upwards.

Braudy emerged from the fog, holding a shovel over his shoulder. Tucker pushed himself up on to his elbows. He said, 'Tom's been a silly boy. He fell over.'

'He fucking attacked me.'

'No-one gives a shit, Tom.'

Braudy touched the gauze in his ear and looked around. He squinted into the fog. 'Those some trees over there?'

'Aye.'

'Far enough away from the road, aren't we?'

'Yeah.'

'Get up, Tom. Start digging over there. Make the holes six feet long, three feet wide. Four feet deep,' said Braudy. 'Then we can go home.'

'Three holes, Tom,' said Tucker. 'Make sure they're nice and neat.'

Braudy took a sandwich out of the plastic bag. He unwrapped it and screwed the foil into a little ball.

'What flavour is it?' asked Tucker.

'Tuna,' said Braudy, pouring himself some coffee.

'Spoils us, doesn't he?'

Tom started to dig, trying to ignore the insults shouted at him.

CHAPTER FOUR

T HEY RETURNED JUST after three in the afternoon.
It was raining. Tom got out of the truck. He did not say
anything to Tucker or Braudy and returned to his caravan.
There was a message pinned to the cupboard. It read: 'Bar at
10 – Frank.' He stuffed his muddy clothes into a plastic bag.
He washed. His hands were marked with blisters and he had
mud in his hair.

He dried himself with the towel, put on clean trousers, a
T-shirt, and a thick black jumper. He made himself a cup of
hot chocolate. It tasted sweet and reminded him of the malted
drinks he used to have as a kid. He made himself a simple
meal from the leftover items in the fridge. It made him feel a
little better. He lay down on the bed and heard the rain rattle
against the windows. Dead leaves and rubbish shifted around
the yard. Animals moved about beneath the caravan. He lay
there a long time. Somewhere between waking and sleep.

It was dark when he opened his eyes. He heard a shout.
The cry of an animal. Something pained and sorrowful. He
peered out of the window, heart beating fast from the surprise.
Static shadows. Darkness. He wiped rocks of sleep from his
eyes. He checked his watch. It was nearly ten. He looked
through his wallet. Money. Cards. The picture of Stephanie.
After a moment of hesitation he hid the photo and the wallet
in one of the drawers close to his bed.

He put on his coat and left the caravan. The air smelled of

fertiliser and burning wood. The back door was locked so he walked around the side of the building. A security light came on and he passed a small coal shed. He looked inside. There was a strong smell of diesel. The brick walls were painted orange. Metal ducts and plastic pipes hung from the ceiling. In the centre of the room, he saw the incinerator. Its front hatch was closed. The control box was mounted on a small wooden post.

Someone coughed behind him. He turned. Tucker was standing there, holding a few pieces of broken furniture under his arm.

'Found the oven, have you?' asked Tucker.

'Oven?'

'Yeah. It's pizza tonight for tea.'

'Really?'

'Fuck off, you twat. Of course there won't be fucking pizza.' He pushed past and opened the incinerator. Tom stepped back from the heat and watched Tucker throw in the pieces of furniture.

Tom left the coal shed and carried on around the side of the building. He stepped into the lobby of the Bothy and hung up his coat on one of the hooks. There was a scent of air freshener. The bar was clean. A small basket was filled with packets of crisps. Serviettes and cutlery were laid out near the coffee machine.

The fire burned brightly. The fireguard was in place. Frank was sitting on the pool table. He wore neatly pressed trousers and a blazer adorned with shining brass buttons. There were two sovereign rings on the fingers of his left hand. He looked at his watch. 'Right on time.'

'I thought I was late.'

Frank had a few sheets of paper on his knee. It looked like

an itinerary. He fiddled with his silver cufflinks. They were shaped like honeycombs.

'Wayne and his lot should be here soon. From Bradford way.'

'Not that familiar with Bradford,' said Tom.

'Cora's Bradford. She's got webbed toes,' he said, with a smile. 'Keeping her upstairs tonight. Don't want her getting familiar. You know what Bradford people are like.' Frank opened a packet of crisps and offered the bag to Tom. He shook his head and yawned. He realised there were still bits of mud in his hair. Frank had not noticed.

Ken came into the room carrying two trays of freshly made sandwiches cut into neat triangles. The crusts had been removed. The trays were covered with cling film.

'Where do you want these, Frank?' he asked.

'Did you put any salad in them?'

'Should I have done?'

'Fuck no. Put them over there.'

Ken put the sandwiches down. He was wearing an apron over a suit two sizes too small. He fiddled with his cuff-links. They resembled Strepsils.

'Just telling Tom it isn't always easy living out here,' said Frank.

'Too right.'

'You can't stay in your caravan. Pulling yourself off over a Littlewoods catalogue. Thinking of home.'

'Won't get far if you think of home,' said Ken. 'You need mental reserves.'

'Couple of years ago, when we were stuck out here with the snow, Ken here built a model church out of matchsticks. Just to keep his mind straight. Didn't you, Ken?'

'It was a cathedral.'

'Which one?' asked Tom.

'Canterbury.' He took out a small tube of cream and rubbed it on to his cold sore.

'You ever do anything like that? Airfix?'

'I made a spitfire once,' said Tom. 'I wasn't very good at it.'

'Fiddly those things,' said Frank.

'My girlfriend used to make models at home. Stuff from clay.'

'Pots and that?'

'Little statues,' replied Tom. 'People.'

Frank stood up and hitched at the waistband of his trousers. He was wearing a tan belt with a buckle shaped like the white rose of York. Frank brushed at his arms. He picked a piece of white cotton from his shoulder. 'What did Braudy say to you earlier? About the holes.'

'Told me we had to dig three of them,' said Tom.

'Only three?'

'Was that too many?'

'Too few. Fucking Braudy. Shit for brains can't count.'

'No eye for detail,' said Ken.

'I'll tell you, Tom. This place. Herding cats,' sighed Frank. 'Ken. Find an apron for the lad.'

Tom was handed an apron. It was blue gingham. He tied the strings around his waist and heard the growl of diesel engines. The flat, wet sound of tyres running over tarmac.

'Go and get Braudy and Tucker,' said Frank.

Ken left the room.

Frank went over to the window and checked his watch. 'Three minutes late. Not like them.'

'Weather's bad,' said Tom.

'He should have taken that into account.'

Tucker walked in wearing a black patch over his lazy eye. His beige chinos were stained with ketchup and soot. He sat down at a table and lit a cigarette. He pulled a glass ashtray towards him.

'Incinerator done?' asked Frank.

'Junior over there thought we were having pizza,' said Tucker.

Frank finished the crisps, licked his fingers clean, and threw the crisp packet into the bin. Braudy came in, nursing his right hand. It was bandaged. The dressings were fresh.

Frank went over to the window and watched the four black cars pull into the front yard. They stopped and one man from each car stepped out on to the gravel. They were all dressed in boiler suits and wore thick leather gloves. Tom noticed one of the men carried a heavy green shopping bag.

Exhausted and grimy, the other men scraped their muddy boots on the mat outside the front door and took off their gloves. The first man through the door had wiry blonde hair. His forehead was pock-marked. Eyes hard, mouth small and mean. He carried a black rucksack over one shoulder. He patted Frank on the cheek and the two men shook hands.

'All good, Wayne?'

'Thought there were going to be five holes for us.'

'Cause you any mither?'

'Not much,' he said, stripping off his boiler suit. 'We sorted it.'

Another man came in. He had dark hair flecked with grey. Cold blue eyes. He sat down on the bench and took off his boots. Clods of black mud dropped on to the carpet.

Wayne turned to him and said, 'You check the oil, Nixon?'

'Nah. Sachin's doing it.'

Ken picked up Wayne's boiler suit. He folded it neatly and put it on the counter. He rubbed at his sore lip again.

'Herpes back, Ken?' asked Wayne.

There was laughter. Ken gave a weak smile and squeezed out a beer-soaked bar mat over the sink.

'Fuck. What a night. What a night,' said Wayne. He unzipped the rucksack and pulled out cream-coloured trousers, a white shirt, and a blue wool cardigan. He started to dress.

The man with the shopping bag came in and put it down on the table. He had a crew cut and crooked white teeth. He undressed, threw his boiler suit into the middle of the room, and wandered over to the fire, scratching the inside of his groin. Tucker joined him and shook his hand. The man picked up the fireguard and ran his fingers over the brass filigree.

'How much did this fucking cost?' asked the man. 'Weighs a ton.'

'Few hundred quid. Antique.'

'Bit tacky,' he said. 'Looks like one of them birds.'

The man spat into the fire. He missed and hit the hearth. Frank handed the kitchen roll to Braudy, who tore off a piece and wiped up the phlegm.

Sachin walked in through the door. He had oil on his hands and streaks of mud on his forehead. He shook Ken's hand and sat down on the bench.

'Need a cloth?' asked Ken.

'For what?'

'The oil on your hands.'

'Nah.' Sachin snapped off a stray white thread from his long johns.

Frank tapped Wayne on the shoulder.

'Here - have you met Tom yet?'

'No. I haven't.'

Tom leaned over the bar and shook Wayne's hand. He could smell sweat and cheap aftershave.

Frank touched the sovereign rings on his fingers, and said, 'Lad's up here doing some work for us.'

'You got mud in your hair,' said Wayne. 'Frank too mean to let you have a bath?'

'Didn't have time,' said Tom.

Frank gave a pained smile. He handed a large yellow ashtray over to Tom who emptied it and set it back on the counter.

'How's the business going? One in Stockport, is it?' asked Frank.

'Warehouse is in Stockport. Trade's online nowadays. Bit over my head so Nixon sorts that out now.'

'Step up for you, Nixon. Trading in dildos and plastic dolls,' said Frank with a wink.

'Good money in it,' said Wayne. 'Here. No Cora today?'

'She's sleeping,' said Frank. 'Bit of a fever.'

'Galloway'll be disappointed.'

The man with the crooked teeth looked up. 'Disappointed with what?'

'No Cora.'

'Bring her down, you fucker,' said Galloway.

'Can't. She's sick,' said Frank.

'She can have fucking AIDS for all I care. Let's see her.'

'She stays upstairs, mate.'

Galloway's jaw clenched and he said something under his breath to Tucker. Frank watched them both. He went over to the table and looked inside the green shopping bag.

'We did as you wanted,' said Galloway.

'But you didn't get rid of it?'

'That's your business, mate. Not mine.'

Frank scowled and held the bag out to Tucker. 'Take this to the incinerator.'

'Right now?'

'It'll take you five minutes.'

'Want me to do a count?'

'Nah. No need,' said Frank.

Tucker picked up the bag. There was something wet inside. Galloway drummed his fingers on the table and looked at the grey curtains hanging from the broken fittings.

'Just going for a piss,' said Tom.

'Make it quick,' replied Ken.

Galloway and Tucker watched him leave the room. He went to the bathroom. As he pissed, he looked at the black-and-white photograph above the urinal. The woman looked unhappy. He did not know if the sadness was posed or if it was real. He finished, splashed his face with water, and returned to the bar.

'Drink, Wayne?' asked Frank.

'You still have that bitter?'

'Got a new barrel in last week.'

'I'll have some of that. Lads? Beer?'

There were nods around the room.

'Do the honours, Tom,' said Frank. 'Not too much head if you please.'

Tom poured out a pint of beer. The froth looked like sea foam whipped up on a stormy day. He thought he could see small objects floating in the dark liquid. The smell of yeast and hops was strong and made him feel hungry. He poured out another pint and put it on the bar. Wayne put a pound in the collection box.

Frank looked at his watch. 'What's taking that prick Tucker?'

'Want me to go and find him?' asked Ken.

'No. You sit tight.' Frank handed Wayne one of the pints.

Wayne held the glass up to the light and nodded, He downed the pint in one. The beer dribbled down his chin and dripped on to his shirt. He put the glass down.

'Another please, young man.'

While Tom refilled Wayne's glass, he noticed a small wooden carving of a greyhound next to the sink. The brass plaque read 'Biddy's Bureau. Towcester 2000'. Ken patted the carving and said, 'Good dog, that one.'

'What happened to him?'

'Her. She ended up with a family in Rochdale.'

Braudy collected the boiler suits from the middle of the room. He placed them neatly on the bar. Then he collected the men's damp boots and put them near the fire to dry them out. He sat down again and lifted the bandage and touched his injured hand.

Wayne handed Tom his empty glass and said, 'Let me try another.'

'Which? Porter? Pilsner?'

'Porter's good,' said Frank.

'Make it a pilsner.'

Tom poured out a pint and Wayne tasted it. He nodded in approval. 'Nice finish. Would be good with a curry. Something with a bit of spice.'

Frank clicked his fingers at Tom. 'Here. Pass us those pickled eggs.'

'New batch, Frank?'

'Made a few jars in November.'

Tom brought over the jar and watched the eggs bob up and down like sightless eyeballs. Wayne smiled and licked his lips. He unscrewed the lid and picked out an egg. There was a whiff of vinegar and sulphur. As he chewed at it slowly, his eyes watered. Frank reached into the jar and took out an egg. He bit into it and looked at the yolk. He spat into the ashtray.

'What's wrong?' asked Wayne.

'Tastes funny.' Frank rinsed his mouth out with his pint.

Wayne took out another egg and bit into the white. He showed the grey-green yolk up for Frank to see. 'That's bang on. Perfect.'

'You don't have to eat it, mate.'

'Delicious as ever. You're being too hard on yourself.'

Tucker returned from outside. His fingers were blackened with soot. He sat down next to Galloway and handed him a small piece of paper. They both smirked and looked at Tom. It was still raining. Every now and then the lights would flicker and the men would stop talking. When the lights became steady again the talking and laughter resumed as if nothing had happened.

'Give me one of those cigars,' said Frank. 'Just at the back there.'

A wooden box of cigars sat beneath the board filled with postcards and foreign currency. Tom handed the box to Frank who took out a cigar and sniffed it. He lit it and the end of the cigar glowed. He puffed out jags of thick, grey smoke.

'What kind are they?' asked Wayne.

'Cuban.'

'Aye. But what make?'

'Montecristo. Numero – er – four.'

'Novice smoke,' said Wayne, taking out a cigar out of the box. He lit it and weighed the Dupont lighter in his hand.

'Few years old now,' replied Frank.

Wayne sparked the lighter and looked at the flame. 'It's a nice thing, isn't it?'

'Aye. And not a plastic BIC you can walk off with,' said Frank. He held out his hand and Wayne gave the lighter back.

Frank smiled with pride and rapped on the counter with his knuckles. 'Here. Tom. Pick up them boiler suits and take them to the incinerator.'

'Okay.'

'Shouldn't take you five minutes.'

Tom put on a coat and picked up the boiler suits. He stepped outside into the drizzle. He passed the parked cars and made his way to the side of the building. The security light came on. He reached the coal shed and ducked inside. He threw the muddy boiler suits into the incinerator. There was a smell of burning cotton and singed hair.

He stepped outside again and heard a rhythmic banging sound over the wind. Hammering. He pulled up the collar of his coat and moved back towards the front of the Bothy. He walked close to the black cars. One of them had a smashed brake light. Tom took a closer look. The body work was damaged. He saw a hole the size of a penny. He squinted and saw three other holes. All exactly the same size.

Tom took off his coat in the lobby. Rubbing gooseflesh from his arms, he waved Frank over.

'Problems?' asked Frank.

'You might want to tell the guys that one of their cars has some damage.'

'What kind of damage?'

'A few holes.' Tom pointed out the car to Frank.

Frank put his cigar down in the ashtray. He marched over to Wayne and tapped on his shoulder. 'You told me everything went smoothly.'

'It did,' said Wayne.

Frank said, 'Your fucking car got dinged. How's that smooth?'

'Dinged? What the fuck's a ding?'

'A dent, you prick.'

'So what?'

'It means you hit something,' shouted Frank. 'Means you've drawn attention to yourself.'

'We weren't fucking followed, were we?'

'It's the fucking details, Wayne. The fine fucking margins.'

Wayne stood up and clicked his fingers at Ken. 'You. Apron,' he said. 'Come with me.'

Ken stepped from behind the counter and followed Wayne out into the front yard.

Frank returned to Tom's side and looked out of the window. After a few moments, he turned to Tom and said, 'Why don't you knock off early? Turn in. Have a rest.'

'Sure?'

'Ken's got it covered.'

Tom put his coat on and left the bar through the front door. He saw Ken and Wayne. Running their fingers over the holes in the bodywork of the damaged car.

Tom heard the hammering again. He passed by the coal shed. There was a smell of cooking meat. The security light clicked on. As he drew closer to the back of the building, the banging grew louder. He peered into the darkness and scanned the shadows for movement. He could see the skips, the piles of tyres, the fishing boat. Then he saw the source of the noise. It was his caravan. The door was wide open, blown back and forth on its hinges by the wind.

He ran over to the caravan. He looked inside and switched on the lights. The cupboards were open. Muddied clothes were strewn across the floor. The mattress was upside down, the sleeping bag turned inside out. His mobile phone was smashed. He ran over to the drawer where he had put his wallet. His money and his card was there. But the photo of Stephanie was not.

CHAPTER FIVE

T OM SEARCHED THE caravan for the photograph. He
looked under the mattress. In the cupboards and drawers.
The lavatory. Under the folding dining table. He could not
find the photo anywhere. He lay on the bed and looked at the
black sky through the grimy window. Angry, drunken shouts
echoed amongst the outbuildings. Smashing glass. A loud
bang. He put his head under the pillow and closed his eyes.

He woke up at dawn and looked for the photograph again.
No luck. He left the caravan. The clouds were the colour of
margarine. Tom went behind the store to the wood pile. The
tarpaulin flapped in the chilly wind. Someone had already
stripped the Christmas tree of its branches and chopped the
trunk into foot-long sections. He picked up a couple of the
cut pieces and tucked them under his arm.

The cars were no longer in the front yard. Only Frank's
red truck remained. Tom entered the Bothy through the front
door. There was the tang of stale urine. He saw that someone
had used the umbrella stand as an impromptu latrine. He
stepped over the crushed domes of pickled eggs. Broken glass
crunched beneath his feet. The furniture, so neatly arranged
before, was now scattered and smashed. On the bar, there was
a row of glasses filled with cloudy water. Frank's belt was on
the carpet. Tom picked it up and saw there was an inscription
on the buckle. It read: 'English by birth, Yorkshire by the
grace of God'.

Someone groaned. There was a cough and then a single shouted word. Tom saw a figure lying on the pool table. It was Ken. His cufflinks had been removed. A penis had been crudely sketched on to his forehead with a red biro, and a purple bruise had bloomed around the socket of his right eye. Stepping too close, Tom caught the ripe, sweet smell of vomit.

Tom rested a piece of wood on the low fire and made sure the flames caught. He went back into the lobby and carefully moved the umbrella stand outside. He tipped the contents of the stand into the drain. When he returned indoors, he saw Cora was standing near the fire. She wore a dress patterned with cowboys. He watched as she reached up and pushed one of the horse brasses so it was off-centre.

'What happened here?' she asked.

'Did you hear anything last night?'

'I took a sleeping pill. Didn't want any part of it,' she said, sniffing the air. 'Is that piss?'

'Yeah.'

'Is there any air freshener behind the bar?'

Tom looked in the cupboards and found a can of deodorant. He sprayed it around the room. The smell was cloying and unpleasant. Cora tried to open one of the windows. It was stuck. She gave up, sat at the bar, and sprayed the deodorant again. She lit a cigarette and wandered over to the fire. She jabbed at the logs with a brass poker. 'How long have you been up?'

'Not long.'

'What happened to Ken?'

'No idea,' said Tom. 'Don't think that table will be much good for pool.'

Cora plucked out a newspaper from the kindling basket.

She unfolded a page and held it across the front of the fireplace. An updraft made the fire roar. She took the page away, screwed it up, and threw it in to the flames.

'Take it you didn't get involved last night,' she said, spraying the deodorant again. 'Eau D'Ken.'

'Better than piss.'

'A bit.' She took a drag of her cigarette. The smoke caught the back of her throat and she coughed. 'Bollocks.'

'Did you see Frank about?'

'Probably take him a couple of hours to wake up yet. When he does, best keep your head down. He'll be in a shit mood.'

'Hungover?'

'His are the worst. This won't fucking help.' Cora looked at the squashed eggs on the floor and the smashed pickling jar. She hitched her skirt and knelt down. She reached up to the counter for some kitchen roll and started to clear up the mess.

'There's a brush and a mop around the corner,' she said. 'Back there.'

Tom filled a bucket with hot water and detergent and mopped up the vinegar. He watched her pick up the eggs, wrapping each one in paper before dropping it in the bin. She never looked up. He refocused on the cleaning and listened to the rhythmic lick of the mop, the scratch of broken glass on the floor. Cora got to her feet and selected a pool cue from the rack. She poked Ken with it. He moaned and muttered something under his breath. Cora put the pool cue down.

'Not often he gets like this,' she said. 'Usually happens whenever Frank gives him some attention. Makes him feel important. Makes him feel as if he's been forgiven.'

'What did he do?'

'Depends on who you talk to. Some people say he lost the

truck keys. Some say he didn't laugh at one of Frank's jokes. Others say he bought the wrong kind of oven chips.'

'Serious?'

'Nah. Think it was something to do with Frank's ex-wife.'

'Which one?'

'Second and third. Mandy. It's like Burton and Taylor all over again. She left last summer. Couldn't take it up here any more. Went back to Leeds.'

'Braudy said she went back to Liverpool.'

'Well. I heard different.'

'Why did she leave?'

'Why does anyone leave? She'd probably had enough. Twenty years and two marriages was too much. Don't blame the poor cow. He wanted to run things from up here. Up in the fresh air. Away from Leeds. The usual sort of trade for a man like him.'

'Meaning?'

'Use your imagination, Tom.'

Cora lit another cigarette. The smoke made her left eye flicker. She pulled a hankie from her sleeve, and sneezed twice. 'I've been up here too long.'

'Would you leave?'

'Question I ask myself a lot,' she said. 'Truth is I have nowhere else to go. Home is fucked. Boyfriend's houses are fucked. Boyfriends are fucked. Best I can say about Frank? He's never laid a finger on me.'

Tom went back to mopping. He heard Ken say something in his sleep again.

'I was never bored before I came here. Spent a lot of time trying not to get robbed, or murdered. Never boring. But here? With Frank? Bored all the fucking time. Bored out of my fucking tree. And this isn't a dull Sunday afternoon. Or a fucking Ed Sheeran song. This is something else.'

'I can cope with boredom,' said Tom.

She leaned on the counter. 'I saw Tucker leave your caravan last night. While you were still working.'

'Tucker?'

'What was he after? Some booze? Money?'

'A photograph of my girlfriend.'

'What did he want with that?'

'Think he handed it to one of the guys. Galloway.'

She puffed out her cheeks. 'If it's Galloway, you need to tell Frank. Trust me.'

Tom shook his head. 'I don't think that would help.'

'It bloody will,' said Cora. 'And Galloway knows people. If you're in trouble—'

'It might just have been Tucker. Mucking about.'

'Was the photo important?'

Tom nodded and squeezed the mop down into the bucket. He looked at the glint of broken glass on the wet floor. Cora ran her fingers through her hair. It looked glossy in the low light. She rubbed her finger across the wooden counter. Some of the varnish flaked away under her fingernails. Tom placed the mop back in the bucket and looked at the green phone hanging from the wall. He wanted to ask Gary what he should do.

Cora gave a gentle smile. 'Why don't I mention it to Frank? Explain it for you.'

'Why would you do that?'

'Galloway's a right bastard. And besides, I reckon you and me are in the same boat. More or less.' She stubbed out her cigarette and left the room.

Tom carried on cleaning where he could. He wiped down the fridge and saw a plate of sandwiches hidden on a shelf beneath the counter. Although the sandwiches did not look appetising, he was hungry enough to eat. He peeled away the clingfilm, picked up a sandwich, and lifted the corner to see what the filling was. Cheese. Or something like cheese. He ate a couple of sandwiches, scraping the mushed white bread from the roof of his mouth. He switched on the coffee machine and waited for it to brew a fresh pot. He sprayed the deodorant again. Ken moved on to his side and curled up.

Tom threw another log on to the fire and sat down by the front window. After a cup of black coffee, Tom piled up the broken pieces of furniture near the front door. He heard hinges squeak. Frank appeared from the office, holding a damp facecloth to his forehead.

'Ken, you lazy fuck,' he said. 'Get up from there. Jesus.'

Ken stirred and then fell gracefully from the pool table. Frank stormed past, kicked at Ken's ribs, and put the facecloth down on the bar. He looked around the room. The chipped woodwork. The splashes on the wall and carpet. The stained curtains.

'Those fucking pricks.' He reached up, and moved the crooked horse brass back to its original position. He looked at the plate of sandwiches and asked, 'What flavour are these? Brie?'

'Dairylea,' said Tom.

'Close enough.' Frank picked up a sandwich and ate it. 'Those fucking pricks.'

'It's not so bad.'

'The room isn't what they fucked, Tom. They fucked the job.'

'How do you know?'

'They were shot at. And if they were shot at, then someone saw them. And if they were seen, then they fucked up.' Frank sat down and ate another sandwich.

Over Frank's shoulder, Tom could see the stooped figure of Ken leaning against the pool table, retching hard. A string of drool spooled out from his slack mouth.

'What's he doing now?' asked Frank, eyes tightly closed.

'He's – uh – he's just gathering himself.'

'Dick,' said Frank, turning. 'Ken, you're a fucking dick. Where are your keys?'

Ken retched and asked, 'For the truck?'

'What do you fucking think?'

Ken looked about for the keys and Tom saw them sitting under the bench. He picked them up. Frank took the keys off Tom and said to Ken, 'Get yourself cleaned up, and tidy this place. Tom and me are going out for a drive.'

Tom and Frank took the truck. Frank wound down the window and breathed in the cold air. He was pale. They drove over the hilly roads. Past fields that rolled downwards towards the base of a valley. Here and there, Tom caught glimpses of distant reservoirs and clusters of trees.

It took them thirty minutes to reach the lay-by where Tom had parked a day earlier. Tom saw a couple of the 'Butty Van' signs posted along the grass verge. Frank stopped the truck and they climbed out. The clouds were low and dark. The sun milky and indistinct. Tom heard the faint moan of a distant airplane over the rising wind.

Frank went over to the wooden fence and vomited. He put his hands on his hips. Coughing, he pulled on some leather gloves and a red bobble hat. He leaned down to retch once more. Still bending down, he said, 'Be a lad, Tom. Get a shovel. From the back.'

They followed a trail that led up a shallow slope. Small rocks lay scattered on the grass. The soft tufts of heather smelled sweet. Ahead, green hills were bunched into ruffles, forming a rough and indelicate seam with the grey horizon.

Frank slowed down and turned to Tom. 'Which way did you come yesterday, Tom?'

'Hard to tell. Lower down, I think.'

Frank shook his head. 'Shouldn't have sent you out with those boys. Shouldn't have done it. Cora tells me they stole from you.'

Tom said nothing.

'If they stole from you, Tom, I want you to tell me about it.'

'They took one thing.'

'Money?'

'No. It was a photo.'

'Of what?'

'My girlfriend.'

Frank stopped. 'Be honest with me, Tom. Do you need this sorting?'

'I just want the photo back.'

'Those boys have been causing me trouble for a long time now,' he said. 'Fucking about. Not paying attention to details.'

He started to walk again, fists clenched. As they crested the hill, Tom saw where he had worked the day before. Overnight, it had become waterlogged. Thin strands of grass poked out from silvery puddles. The three holes Tom had helped dig the previous day were partially filled with soil and rainwater.

'Thought Wayne had dug two more holes,' said Tom.

'So did I,' said Frank. 'How deep were those holes you did?'

'Three or four foot.'

'Fuck sake.'

As Tom drew closer to the holes, he saw something shining in the grass. It was a beer can. Frank picked it up, disgusted. Tom saw something else. It was a blue object, sticking out of one of the holes. Clothes. A coat, a jacket. Denim. Frank had seen it too.

They stood over a man who had managed to struggle halfway out of one of the holes. Blood had blackened the collar of his jacket and his arms reached out over the soil. The soft ground was furrowed from the man's desperate clawing. His right hand was encrusted with dark mud. His left hand had been cut off.

'Out of the way, Tom.' Frank calmly lifted the man up by the hair. 'No fucking idea who this bozo is. Not the man I wanted, that's for sure.'

'What about the – uh – the other holes?'

Frank held his hand up for silence. He took off his bobble hat, put it in his pocket. Tom watched him for a few moments. He could hear something. The half-buried man gurgled and let out a pained groan.

'Frank! He's still alive!'

'Fuck sake,' said Frank.

The man, through desperate breaths, was trying to say something.

'It'll be okay,' said Tom, kneeling down and reaching for the man's right hand.

'Stand back, Tom,' said Frank.

'I'll dig him out.'

Frank stood over the gasping, half-buried man and raised his foot. He stamped on the man's head. He kept stamping, and only stopped when the man's head was no longer the right shape. Tom's knees felt weak. He didn't want to see it. He didn't want to hear it. He turned away and was sick. First into his hands, and then on to the ground.

Frank looked at the dead man in front of him. He wiped his feet on the grass. Tom looked up at him.

'Get up,' said Frank. 'Bury him properly. Bury them all properly.'

Long shadows fell across hills and rocks. A distant forest appeared black against the sky. The grass and heather glistened softly with dew. Tom limped along. His trousers were slick with dirt, his shirt spattered with brains and blood. His hands were sore from digging and he could not stop his mind from slipping back to the moments when he had thrown earth over the heads of dead men.

Frank was carrying the shovel in one hand. He smoked a cigarette and glanced back at him. 'All right there?' he asked.

'Yeah,' said Tom, pushing past him. Frank put his cigarette out on the sole of his shoe and pocketed the butt.

'Expect you're hungry now,' said Frank. 'Hungry and tired.'

Tom did not hear him. He kept walking.

'We'll get you moved from that caravan. Get something to eat.'

Tom kicked at a stone.

'Hey. I'm talking to you.' Frank shoved Tom in the back and he tripped. He broke his fall with his blistered hands. He sat down and wiped tears from his eyes with a damp sleeve. Frank stabbed his shovel into the ground, and came over to stand next to him. Tom, too weak to defend himself, looked up. His fogged mind tugged him back to the memory of Frank cleaning the blood and brain off his shoes on the grass. The handless arms of the men they had reburied.

Frank grabbed Tom's collar and pulled him to his feet.

'Up. Up. Up.' He seized Tom's jaw. 'You're in this too now, Tom. Don't forget that.'

Tom was released and Frank pulled the shovel from the ground and walked away. Tom traipsed along the path after him and looked at the back of his thick neck. There was a dark birthmark close to the hairline.

He saw other pieces of litter on the ground, snagged on thorny bushes. White polystyrene cartons. Several blue forks, a torn plastic bag that fluttered in the breeze.

They reached the truck. Frank threw the shovel on to the flatbed and opened the driver's door. He reached behind the seat and brought out an empty rubble sack and put it on the ground. He started to unbutton his coat. 'Okay, Tom. Strip.'

'What?'

'Put your clothes in the sack. No sense spreading that dead prick's brains all over the truck too.' Frank unbuttoned his shirt. He untied his shoe laces. He pulled off a boot and looked at it sadly. 'Bloody good these too. Comfy. Shame to get rid of them.'

Tom watched. 'Get rid of them?'

'We'll burn them. Everything except your underpants.' Frank pulled down his trousers. 'If you're desperate, you can borrow some of my clothes,' he said. 'Anyways, we can always get Ken to go and pick something up for you from town.'

Tom took his off jumper. He wheeled his arms around to get some warmth into them.

'Come on lad,' said Frank. 'Quicker you get down to your drawers, the faster we'll be in the truck with the blowers on.'

When Tom was down to his pants he got into the truck. Frank opened the glove compartment. He searched through service manuals, unpaid parking tickets, scratched Yes CDs. He picked out a half-empty miniature bottle of single malt whisky and handed it to Tom.

'Neck that and you'll feel better,' he said.

Frank started the engine and put the heaters on. Tom caught the smell of warm dust and watched frayed cobwebs blow outwards from the grilles.

Tom opened the miniature, wiped the neck of the bottle, and tipped it back. He coughed.

'All of it,' said Frank.

Tom finished the bottle. His eyes watered. Frank eased the truck out on to the road and switched on the headlights.

'Better?' asked Frank.

'Yeah.'

'Look at us. Reduced to this,' said Frank, laughing. 'A right pair. How many layers of pants you wearing there?'

'One. Didn't think we'd be out today.'

'My fault. My fault. Should have warned you.' He looked downwards at his crotch. 'Mind you, not much better with two layers.'

In the growing gloom, Tom watched the clouds skim the hilltops. There was a volley of sleet against the windscreen. Frank blew out his cheeks and shook his head. 'What you saw back there. You know I had to do it, don't you?'

Tom did not answer.

'What you saw,' he said. 'What you saw wasn't my fault. It was all Wayne.'

63

'That man back there hadn't done anything wrong. He was trying to speak.'

'And?'

'I thought we could have helped him.'

'Help him? Lord. No, Tom. No, no. Don't get me wrong: I feel for the guy. I really do. Breaks my heart I had to do that. It wasn't - it was like a duty. A duty to me, the boys, Cora. You. Duty to him, for Christ's sake. If I met him somewhere else - if it was different circumstances - I'd probably have bought him a fucking drink or something. You know?'

Tom put his hands close to the blowers.

'What would we do if we had him in the back now?' asked Frank. 'Bleeding everywhere. What then? Go to hospital where he could say him and his mates were abducted? No. No thanks, Tom. Not something I want to deal with.'

'But—'

Frank smashed his hand down on the steering wheel. 'That cunt Wayne made me do this. Blame him. Not me. And don't think I'm letting any of this go. I paid that mongrel to kill some people. My enemies. And he let them go. Thought he could pull the wool over my fucking eyes. Cunt will pay for what he did to us, to those people.' There was another rattle of sleet and Frank wiped at the fogged windscreen with the back of his hand.

'This fucking weather,' he said. 'This fucking day.'

CHAPTER SIX

THEY ARRIVED BACK at the Bothy. Frank parked close to the entrance. Tom ran across the yard into the small lobby. He held the door open for Frank and went in after him. The warmth of the room tickled his flesh.

Braudy and Tucker sat at one of the tables, leaning back from dinner plates smeared with gravy, soggy pastry, bullet-hard peas. Tucker dabbed cigarette ash into a foil pie tray. He had taken off his patch, and both eyes were a shade of pale yellow. Braudy pushed his plate away with his broken hand. He touched his infected ear and wiped some clear discharge from his fingers.

'What happened to your fucking clothes?' asked Tucker.

'Bit of a fucking mess,' replied Frank. 'Get yourself over by the fire, Tom.'

Tom turned his back to the fire. He tried to rub warmth back into his arms.

Ken was attempting to clean the pool table. His bruised eye was half-closed. The penis drawn on his head was still partially visible.

Frank looked at him, shook his head and said, 'Anyone got a hat for Ken?'

Tucker took a woolly hat out of his pocket and handed it over. Ken put it on and pulled down the seam so it covered his eyebrows and ears. He resumed cleaning the pool table, carefully blotting away the stains and marks with a blue cloth.

Frank leaned against the bar. 'Get Tom a brandy. Lad's earned it today.'

Ken put down his cloth, went behind the bar, and washed his hands.

'Does Tom want a single?' he asked.

'Double,' said Frank.

Tom sat down and shivered. His head ached and his hands shook. His vision was blurred. He was afraid he might cry.

'Frank?' asked Ken.

'So what was the problem?' asked Braudy.

'Did Tom crash the truck or something?' laughed Tucker.

'Wayne hadn't buried the bodies properly,' said Frank. 'One of them was still alive.'

Tucker took a long drag on his cigarette. He exhaled smoke through his nostrils and said, 'So fucking what? Cold would have finished him off.'

'I didn't pay the fucking cold to do Wayne's job for him, did I?' said Frank. 'Besides, they were the wrong men, you thick bastard.'

'Fuckers probably deserved it.'

'Still means I have to go and do the work I fucking paid him for,' shouted Frank. 'You know how much it cost me? Bastard's ripped me off.'

'Told you we should have done it ourselves.'

'This funny to you?'

'Trying not to get carried away, mate. That's all,' said Tucker, looking at his watch.

'Frank?' asked Ken. Only Tom heard him.

Frank clicked his fingers at Braudy. 'You. Go to the caravan and bring in Tom's stuff. He's staying in the house now. And get the lad some shoes.'

Braudy left the room through the back door. He slammed it behind him.

'Frank? A word?' asked Ken.

Frank pointed at Tucker. 'You. There's a rubble sack in the truck.'

'Outside?'

'Fuck sake. Yes. Outside. Take it to the incinerator.'

'The incinerator isn't on.'

'Turn it on, then.'

'Now?'

'What do you fucking think?'

Tucker jabbed out his cigarette in the pie dish. Frank watched him go out of the front door.

Ken put his hand up. 'Frank?'

'What? What the fuck is it?'

Ken took a step back. 'I just wanted to know if Tom wanted ice in his brandy.'

'Fucking ask him, then. Jesus.'

He rubbed his head and said, in a quiet voice, 'Ice, Tom?'

Tom did not hear.

'Ice?'

'Give him ice,' said Frank.

Ken poured out a double brandy and handed it to Tom. He took a sip and let it warm his belly. Slowly, his hands steadied. He watched Frank stride around the bar with his arms held behind his back. Tom finished the brandy. Ken refilled his glass. Braudy came back into the bar carrying Tom's bag and a pair of old black Oxfords. Tom opened his bag and put on jeans and a T-shirt. He pulled out old scrunched-up newspaper from the shoes and squeezed his feet in. The leather bit into the bridge of his foot.

'How are they, Tom?' asked Frank.

'Tight.'

Frank knelt down and prodded at the toes with a thumb. 'Plenty of room. Loosen the laces and walk around a bit. Let your feet stretch the leather.'

Tom left the laces untied and crossed the length of the room. He tried not to hobble. Frank put a hand on Ken's shoulder and said, 'Take Tom to his new room. The ensuite. Tom can have a bath or something. Warm up a bit.'

Tom picked up his rucksack and followed Ken through to the office. They took a door to the right, which led through to a corridor and a warren of half-finished rooms. They passed by a laundry room. An old washing machine and a tumble dryer stood in the corner. Water inlet pipes were held in place with tape and string. A large grey tube ran from the back of the dryer and was nailed to the wall. Grey fur and fluff had gathered around the opening of the vent. A pile of wet floor warning signs sat on a low table with black metal legs. The room smelled of damp and soap powder.

Further down the corridor, Tom saw walls stripped of plaster so only flimsy wooden strips remained. An unopened packet of tongue-and-groove flooring was stacked up in the middle of one room. Inexpertly hung offcuts of floral wall-papers were spotted with mildew. Other walls were faintly marked with the measurements of long-forgotten building projects. Flesh-coloured mushrooms sprouted in shadowed corners.

'Don't touch these walls, Tom,' said Ken. 'They're load-bearing.'

Tom frowned. 'How are they load-bearing if I can't touch them?'

'Something to do with the – you know. The lintels and stuff. Braudy knows better than me.'

They passed a firmly locked metal door. Tom could smell wet concrete. Loose wires hung from exposed ceiling joists.

'This bit is an old part,' said Ken. 'Built for shepherds and what-not.'

There was a small bathroom to the right. Thick streaks of dark mould ran up the wall. The toilet and the sink were close together. Both were made from white ceramic. The linoleum was covered in fine white dust. Tom ducked beneath a rotten beam and Ken pushed open a door, revealing a small, window-less room. Tom caught his leg on an armchair pushed into the corner. Its foam insides poked out from the torn silk covering. He turned on the light. One of the walls was covered with peeling sheets of newspaper. The other three walls were pink. A painting of flying geese hung over the bed. There was a bath with no side panel. He could see dust and mouse droppings beneath dull copper pipes.

'Ensuite,' said Tom.

'Good, isn't it? Have a bath and get straight into bed afterwards.'

Tom sat down and tested the mattress. The bedsprings jangled. There was a small bedside table. It was held together with nails and duct tape. Tom tried to open the drawer but it was stuck.

'There's a knack,' said Ken.

'And what's that?'

'Not sure.'

Tom went over to the bath and turned on the rusty tap. Pipes squeaked and howled. Brown water spurted out. He turned off the tap.

'Best to run the water for a minute before you put the plug in,' said Ken.

'Anything else I need to know?'

'The kitchen's down the corridor. You hungry?'

'A coffee would be better,' replied Tom.

Ken led the way and Tom breathed in the scent of damp and animal fats. He stepped through into the kitchen. Overhead, a fluorescent tube buzzed and filled the room with green-tinged light. There was a small table made from oak. Beneath a window caked in black grease, a Belfast sink was heaped with dirty pots and plates. There was a cooker in the corner. Nearby, an old microwave was pushed up against the wall. Two burly fridge freezers stood near the door. Tom looked inside one. It was empty save for a single banana-flavoured yoghurt. He opened up the other fridge. It contained several pairs of socks. All of different colours and types.

Ken rubbed at his bruised eye and sat down at the table. 'I get hot feet. It's a circulation thing.'

'Right.'

'Pass us a pair.'

Tom handed him a pair of wool socks.

Ken put them on and said, 'You wanted tea, right?'

'Coffee.'

'Cupboard over there.' Ken looked around once more and, satisfied the tour was done, left the room.

Tom switched on the kettle. On the faux marble counter there was a small pile of leather-bound menu covers. Grubby tea towels were stuffed into half-open drawers. The row of cupboards did not quite hang true. One cupboard was crammed with small pots of cloves and thyme. Another contained upturned jars of coffee and a loose assembly of tea bags. Tom picked up one of the coffee jars. He unscrewed the lid, and took a careful sniff. He found a spoon and used it to chisel away at the granules until he was able to tip a good quantity of coffee into the mug along with the boiling water. There was already an open carton of UHT milk. He added some into the cup and watched it cloud the coffee. He gave it a stir and a taste. He sat down at the table and stared at the wall above the cooker. It was stained with droplets of cooking oil and splashes of brown gravy. He picked up one of the menus. He looked through the appetisers, the mains, the puddings. All standard dishes. There was an early-bird special. Two courses for a fiver.

There was a noise. Scratching and skittering claws. He looked downwards to see a mouse clamber over his left shoe and giddily run away from him. Tom watched it press through a narrow crack beneath the sink. With a final shiver of its tail, the mouse squirmed into the darkness and Tom was alone once again.

After finishing his drink he went to his room. He sat on his bed for a while, looking at the newspaper on the walls. The pages were pulled from old tabloids. The bold headlines concerning lurid scandals. Politicians on the fiddle. Nurses on strike. Heart disease. Warnings about foreign footballers. He could smell sweat. Something stale. A hint of drains.

He tried to open the drawer in the bedside table. He gave it a rattle and something wooden snapped. He pulled the whole drawer out and put it down on the bed. He found a torch, a half-open packet of chewing gum, and a matchbook. Stuck to the bottom of the drawer was a small address book. The cover was made from fake red leather. He flicked through. Nothing was written in it but a Polaroid fell out. The picture was of a middle-aged woman. Leathery, tanned skin. She sat on a thin mattress. Her back was up against a yellow wall. Beer cans at her feet. Her hair was dark and straight. Breasts exposed. Legs open. She was not smiling and her eyes were glazed and joyless.

He took the picture into the kitchen and tore it up before throwing it into the bin. He returned to his room and undressed. He did not switch off the light and lay down on the bed, afraid of what he might see once he closed his eyes.

CHAPTER SEVEN

T OM WOKE IN darkness. Sadness and fear welled up inside him. He listened to the sounds of the house and heard far-off voices. Laughter and shouting. He thought of the man in the hole. And then he thought of the others they had reburied. Bullet holes in the backs of their heads. Their left hands missing. Removed as a punishment. Or perhaps as a means of counting. The dead men's mouths contorted from either terror or suffocation. He imagined throwing dirt over them again, covering their faces so they no longer had to look up at the world that had condemned them to such painful deaths. He tried to remind himself that all pain, all suffering, eventually passed. People adapted. Memories faded.

He turned his attention to his sore hands, his stinging skin, his aching joints. He shifted on the mattress and a bedspring poked into his thigh. He smelled something. Coffee. He carefully reached out and touched the bedside table. His fingers brushed against something warm. A cup. He sniffed the drink and took a sip. Lukewarm and sweet. He set the cup down. The coffee warmed him and his thoughts turned to Stephanie. The memory of her was no longer sharp. As he fell asleep he tried to recall her scent. Something like apricots. Something like perspiration.

He stirred from his sleep some hours later and could still smell coffee. The cup was still there. Warmer this time.

Refilled. He sipped at it and lay back on his pillow. His bladder ached. He needed a piss and thought of using the sink, or the bath, but couldn't bring himself to do it. He stood and made his way across the room. Patting the walls on either side of the door he found the light switch, and tried it. There was a flash and a pop. He tried the switch again. No luck. He felt for the door handle, turned it, and stepped out into the corridor. He crossed over to the toilet opposite, closed the door, and batted helplessly at the pull switch before catching it. He pulled it and the string snapped. He put the string on the floor and moved towards the toilet. He touched the seat and sat down, unwilling to trust his aim in the darkness. He had a piss and washed his hands. He shambled back to his bed and went back to sleep.

When he opened his eyes again, he saw four lines suspended in the dark. Light shining through the cracks of the door frame. There was a creak of hinges, a swear word. The door opened and the light from the corridor hurt his eyes. Tom saw a figure. It was Frank. He was holding a mug. Steam rose from it.

'You awake?' he asked.

Tom yawned. 'Yeah. Yeah.'

Frank tried the light switch.

'Bulb's gone,' said Tom.

Frank put the cup down on the bedside table. Tom saw him move back towards the door. In the half-light he saw Frank's profile. Its points, its lines. Tom pushed himself up on to his elbows and looked at the cup. Coffee, again.

'How long have I been out?'

'Couple of days.'

'Shit.' Tom took a sip from the cup. The coffee was sweet.

Frank leaned his back against the doorframe, and lit a cigarette, gesturing up to the light. 'Fuses had gone. Ken noticed when he dropped off your laundry.'

'He washed my clothes?'

'Yeah. They should be here somewhere. Hang on.' He looked around and left the room. Tom heard scrabbling and wheezing. Frank returned with a small pile of folded laundry. 'Wrong door,' he explained, cigarette hanging from his mouth. 'Where do you want them?'

'I dunno. Just there?'

Frank dropped the clothes on top of his bag. 'Your friend phoned up. Gary. Mind if I sit?'

Tom yawned again. 'Go ahead.'

Frank pulled out the silk-covered chair sitting at the foot of the bed. He tested the surface with his hand, and sat down. 'He called last night.'

'You should have come to get me.'

'Nice to have chatted with him, to be honest.'

'What did he say?'

'Not much has changed at home,' said Frank.

'Not much?'

'It hasn't changed for the better. Still problems with the girlfriend's family. What's her name again?'

'Stephanie.'

'Aye. Stephanie. Still no improvement.'

'None at all?'

'Short term, no,' said Frank.

'What about long term?'

'He has no idea. Seemed to think you'd have to wait and see. Keep your head down.'

'Is he okay?'

'Put out, I think. Not that you can be blamed for Steph's family—'

'Stephanie.'

'Can't pick the family, can you?' Frank stubbed out his cigarette on the wall. 'Know you've been through a lot. And that carries its own weight, doesn't it? Consequences matching the causes and what have you.'

'I didn't do anything wrong.'

Frank shook his head. 'You wouldn't be here if Stephanie's family cared about that. You have to live the life of a guilty man now. Like the rest of us.'

Tom looked at the laundry at the foot of the bed. Three black socks on the top of the pile. No sign of the fourth.

'Had a chat with the boys,' said Frank. 'Tucker owned up to stealing that photo of yours. Told me he was messing around. Stole it and was going to do something to it. Like – I dunno – stick it on a picture of a page three model or something.'

'So where is it?'

'He panicked and burnt it in the incinerator.'

'He burned it?'

'Yeah.'

'That was the only picture I had,' said Tom.

'It's gone,' shrugged Frank.

Tom put his coffee down on the bedside table, and folded his arms. He studied Frank's face for a moment. The narrow eyes and weak chin. The thin lips.

Frank picked at his ear and said, 'I promise, Tom. You won't hear – you won't get any more shit about this.'

'If I do?'

'You won't. Get some rest.'

Another day passed. A bitter wind blew in from the north. There were clouds over the hills and the air was colder than the day before. Mists hung over some of the peaks. It started to rain just before midday so Tom stayed indoors and played pool for a while. He racked the balls on the black spot. The nap of the baize was still matted in places from Ken's vomit. Tom broke the pack and slowly moved around the table, going for difficult shots, partly because he wanted to avoid the tear in the playing surface. He found a cube of blue chalk resting on one of the radiators. He chalked his cue and tried a few trick shots, none of which came off. Now and then, he heard a few bikers roar past. There were a couple of cars, ferrying walkers and fell runners around from one route to the next. Never slowing down when they passed the Bothy.

Tom cleared the table and restored the cue to the rack and put the chalk on the cushion. He looked at the golf and darts trophies that sat on the shelf. He found a cloth and dusted them, being careful not to dislodge the flimsy plastic figures glued to the top of each trophy. After he had done that, he switched on the television. The picture fizzed with static. One half of the screen was burned in and brightly coloured spots appeared in the top right-hand corner. He moved the makeshift antenna about, hoping to see a picture through the fizzing noise. He thought he saw some horse racing but soon gave up and switched off the television.

Tucker came into the bar. Tucker was wearing a body warmer and cargo trousers. His orange T-shirt was dirty and faded. He was wearing his eyepatch. His right hand was bandaged and he had a cut on the side of his cheek. He poured himself a vodka and threw in a handful of ice and a thick slice of lemon. He gave it a stir and put a straw into the glass. His one good eye was yellow and bloodshot. He picked up a packet of crisps and a large black ashtray. He sat with Tom and split open the bag of crisps. 'Thought we were out of crisps. Dozy cunt Ken keeps forgetting to buy them. Want one?'

'No.'

'Not a crisp fan?'

'Sometimes,' said Tom.

'Good with a drink.'

'Are you guys busy at the moment?'

'Yeah. Have to sort out these men in Oldham,' he said, taking out a pouch of tobacco. He rolled a cigarette and lit it. 'Can't complain. Nice to be busy. Can get awful lonely up here. Awful.'

'I heard about the winters.'

'Heard? You're in one. This is what it's like. Fuck-all going on. No-one around. Rain outside. No life. No excitement. Just drudgery.'

'Could be worse.'

'How?'

'Could be cold. Hungry.'

'You've been talking to Frank too much.' He held up his bandaged hand. 'But then you're a bit of a favourite up here. Aren't you?'

'I don't know.'

Tucker blew out smoke and smiled. 'I've been told to lay off you. Stop stealing your stuff.'

'I'm not falling for that again.'

'What do you mean?'

'Last time you told me you were going to lay off—'

'Mean it this time. Water under the bridge,' he said. 'Come on. Let's make nice. Have a crisp.'

Tom picked up a crisp and ate it. It was stale.

'That was the last picture I had of her.'

Tucker put his cigarette into his mouth and searched his pockets. He took out a photo of a girl lying on a bed. She had a pair of nylon stockings wrapped around her throat. 'Would this fill the gap?'

Tom shook his head.

Tucker pulled a strand of tobacco from his tongue and took a sip of his vodka. He smiled. 'Frank used to bring women up here. Ones from Manchester, Liverpool. Class birds. Some from Leeds. Sheffield. Nice girls. All sit on your lap and laugh at your jokes. Not all they did, of course. Broke a bed with one of them. Think she was called Denise. Small tits. Big arse. From Bolton. You ever been over that way?'

'Not to Bolton.'

'Good chip shops.' Tucker tapped the ash from his cigarette. 'Nah. We used to get loads of people up here. Guys running drugs, guns. Everything. Know where you sleep now? Where there are all those half-built rooms?'

'Yeah.'

'That was supposed to be bedrooms for another five or six guys.'

'They used to stay there?'

'You're the first one we've had up here in a while. Why we weren't sure about you. It's not like Frank has plenty of money to pay people wages.'

'I'm not being paid. If that helps.'

Tucker put his cigarette out in the ashtray and chewed at his thumbnail. 'We don't get pay rises no more. We don't eat fish on Fridays. We don't get milk delivered up here. Even though there's a dairy farm a few miles down the fucking road.'

'Not many places for fish,' said Tom.

'Grimsby isn't far.' Tucker lifted his eyepatch and blinked. 'Used to get in some nice cod. Megrim. Ever have that?'

'No.'

'You can't beat a bit of Megrim. Yeah. Always had fish on a Friday. Kept us healthy,' said Tucker. 'Frank blames Cora, of course. How she doesn't like fish. How she doesn't like milk.'

'Doesn't she?'

'It was better when Mandy was here.'

'Frank doesn't like talking about her, does he?'

Tucker put his eyepatch back on. 'Word is Mandy cheated on him.'

'I thought she left.'

'She did. Went back to Blackpool.'

'Cora told me it was Leeds.'

'It was Blackpool,' said Tucker. 'You don't stick around if you cross someone like Frank.' He stretched and picked up his tobacco pouch. 'Finish them crisps if you like. They're a bit soft. Past their sell-by.'

CHAPTER EIGHT

I N   T H E   K I T C H E N, Tom found a loaf of white bread hidden away in a cupboard filled with tins of soup. He found a couple of slices that weren't mouldy and toasted them under the grill. The element heated up and he could smell hot oil. He put the kettle on and brewed a cup of strong tea. He took the toast out and scraped the burnt bits into the bin. There was no butter so he ate the toast as it was and listened to the refrigerators hum. He made himself another tea and, as the kettle came to the boil, he heard voices come down the corridor. Near one of the fridges, another small brown mouse ran towards a gap in the wall. It stopped, scratched its nose, and squeezed into the crack.

Tom washed up his cup and left the kitchen. He walked past the room with the metal door. It was locked. He carried on through to the bar. The front door was lodged open. There was a smell of dust and woodsmoke. Frank was sitting at the bar smoking a cigarette. He wore a suit and tartan slippers. He was writing down a list on a torn piece of butcher's paper with a pencil. It had a small pink rubber on the end. Frank picked up a full ashtray and tipped the cigarette butts into the bin behind the bar. He washed the ashtray in the sink.

'Think you might have mice,' said Tom.

'Bound to in an old house like this.'

'There might be a few. In the walls.'

'Where?'

'Kitchen.'

'I'll get Ken to put some traps down,' he said. Frank put down his pencil and looked over at Tom.

'I don't mind helping.'

'Leave it for now. We've got a big day ahead of us. Mice can be sorted later,' he said. 'Not having a good week so far, Tom. Five grand poorer. Made to look like a dopey prick by that piece of shit Wayne. And still have my enemies wandering around in sunny Oldham. Look a bit daft now, don't I?'

'Sure people don't think like that.'

'Can't afford to look soft, Tom. Not any more.'

Outside, the clouds were low and dark. The truck was parked up close to the store. Frank went back to his list, wrote something down, and opened the front door. Tucker and Braudy came in carrying big metal toolboxes. They set the boxes down on the pool table. Braudy had caught his hand on something and small beads of blood appeared on the end of his podgy finger. He sat down by the fire and dabbed at the cut with a torn paper tissue.

Frank consulted the piece of butcher paper. He traced down the list with his index finger and said, 'What have you got in there?'

'Ropes and nail guns. Vices,' said Braudy.

Frank tapped an item on his list. 'Hammers?

'Club,' said Tucker, setting down the toolbox on the pool table. He opened the lid.

'I don't need to see it,' said Frank. 'I just need you to get it right.'

'What about a claw hammer?'

'Stick to the list,' said Frank. 'Bring in some paint cans when you're done.'

'How many?'

'Two.'

Braudy and Tucker lifted up their toolboxes. They left the room, grunting with effort.

Frank got up from the bar and threw a log on to the fire. He breathed out deeply and rubbed at his eyes. 'Running things,' he said, sitting down again. 'Hard when they don't think for themselves. Even harder when they do.'

He picked up his pencil and added another item to the list.

'Are you sure I can't help?' asked Tom.

Frank stopped writing, opened a drawer, and took out the small notebook used to record the oil tank measurements. He pushed the book over to Tom and went back to his list.

After finding a tape measure, Tom went out to the back yard. The weather was getting colder. It started to rain. Muddy curtains stirred in the broken windows of the older caravan. A smashed pane of glass rested on top of a skip. Stepping around the oily puddles, he undid the valve on the oil tank and took the measurement. He climbed down from the tank and strolled around the building, passing the hatch that led to the cellar. Tucker and Braudy were arguing near the store.

Back in the bar, Tom was relieved to find Frank was no longer there. He put the book of measurements back in the drawer behind the counter. He saw there were a couple of old magazines lying around. He read them at the table near the front windows. They were filled with tedious articles and film reviews. There was an account of someone's ideal weekend. An interview with a dead-eyed actor promoting a TV series. Unheralded; long forgotten. He turned to the back pages, and did the crosswords, the puzzles. Adding horns and black teeth to the pictures of grinning celebrities.

An hour later, Ken came in, wiping oil from his hands. He wore the bobble hat again. It was pulled down over his forehead. He took out a small tube from his pocket and smeared some cream on to his cold sore. He switched on the lights and took off his shoes and socks. Behind the bar, he filled a blue washing-up bowl with hot water and washing-up liquid. He set it down on the carpet and dipped his feet into the bowl. He sighed with relief.

'You should get one of those foot spa things,' said Tom.

'Do they still make them?'

'My girlfriend's mum had one.'

'I remember my granny having one. Made a funny noise when you switched it on.'

'Ever try it out?'

'Not hygienic to use someone else's foot spa.' Ken massaged his feet and soapy water sloshed out on to the carpet. 'Nah. This is just right. A pair of clean socks later on and that'll do me nicely.'

Braudy walked in from the office. He was carrying a cup of Dettol, some cotton wool, a box of plasters. A roll of surgical tape.

'How's the ear, Braudy?' asked Ken.

'Worse.'

'You need antibiotics.'

'Can't. I'm allergic to them.' Braudy removed the plaster from his ear. He took out the wadding and examined it. It was sticky from the discharge. He tore off a fresh piece of cotton wool, dipped it in the cup of Dettol, and dabbed gently at his ear while he watched the rain.

'I heard olive oil is good for ears,' said Ken.

Braudy grimaced. 'Olive oil?'

'That's for ear wax,' said Tom. 'When you want to loosen it.'

'Oh.'

'My dad had to do it after he went deaf in one ear. Had it syringed.'

'Did it work?'

'It got rid of the wax,' said Tom, 'but perforated his ear drum.'

'I bet it's an unpleasant feeling,' said Ken. 'Having olive oil in your ear.'

Braudy tore off another cotton bud and put it in his ear. He taped it up, and tipped the cup of Dettol down the sink behind the bar. He threw away the old plaster and the used cotton wool. Tom listened to the rain hammer against the windows.

CHAPTER NINE

TOM SWITCHED ON the light in his bedroom. He went through the pile of washing Ken had done for him. His T-shirts were torn around the shoulders and the arms. He searched through the underpants. None of them were his. Off-white cotton Y-fronts. Superman boxers. A tan jockstrap. The boxers were about his size and he put them on. The elastic waistband was slack. He wondered if they belonged to Ken.

He put on his shoes and stepped into the corridor. Two enormous rolls of white polythene stood outside the room with the metal door. It was unlocked. He poked his head in to the room. It was dark. He tried the light switch, and a naked bulb flickered on to reveal a space only slightly bigger than his bedroom. The walls and ceilings were painted white. A small iron grating was set into the middle of the concrete floor. The two large toolboxes were there, along with three kettles. In the corner, beneath a heavy wooden chair, Tom could see paint cans. The colour was apple white. There were a few rolls of duct tape. Everything was neatly laid out.

Tom left the room. He passed through the office and its shabby gallery of pornographic calendars. The bar was chilly. Ken was sitting at a table near the front window. His bobble hat was pulled low, concealing his eyebrows. His black eye had started to fade. He wasn't wearing any shoes or socks.

There were two small boxes sitting in front of him. One of the boxes had the word 'UNCHECKED' scrawled on its side, in green crayon. The other box had 'REJECT' written on it in black biro. Ken picked out a small object from the 'unchecked' box, and shook it near his ear. He placed it on the table. He repeated the action again. This time, he frowned and dropped the object in the 'reject' box.

Tom waited a moment and then said, 'What did you do with my underpants?'

Ken made a noise in his throat and shook his head. 'Yours the frilly red ones?'

'Did I do something wrong?'

'You got another man to do your washing,' replied Ken.

Tom sat down on the bench. He saw that Frank's truck was no longer in the yard. The winds were strong. The rain cold.

Ken took off his bobble hat. The drawing of the penis was still visible. His forehead was red from scrubbing. He reached into the 'unchecked' box and said, 'Frank should be back by five this evening.'

'What you up to?' asked Tom.

'QA,' he said.

'What?'

'QA. Quality Assurance.'

'For what?'

Ken held out his palm. He was holding a bullet. 'Frank likes having these checked. He bought some ammunition from this Irish or Welsh fella. Bullets were all duds.'

Tom frowned. 'How do you check them?'

'Frank says that if you give them a shake, and you can hear the gunpowder rattle, then it's a dud.'

Tom smiled. 'Are you serious?'

'Yep.'

'That's bollocks.'

87

'What's bollocks?'

'That,' said Tom. 'Listening to bullets.'

'It's true. You just need to know what to listen for.'

Tom laughed.

Ken put a bullet down on the table. 'Since when were you an expert on ordnance?'

'It's not about being an expert.'

'Then you don't know.'

'That's not the point.'

'You don't know. Do you?'

Tom bowed his head, trying not to smile.

'Try it.' Ken handed over a bullet from the 'reject' box. 'This one's a dud.'

Tom held the bullet close to his ear and shook it. He heard nothing, but nodded and handed it back to Ken.

'It sounds like loose sand, doesn't it?' Ken dropped the bullet back in the 'reject' box.

'Do you test those rejects or something?' asked Tom. 'Like try them in a gun to see if the – uh – test is right?'

'No, dickhead,' said Ken. 'Why test the fucking test?'

'Well—'

'Nothing wrong with the test. Important to keep up standards here. Important I can look Frank square in the eye and guarantee that these lot here will work.' He gestured towards the bullets lined up on the table. 'Attention to detail, you see. That's what you need. If you let the little things slip, then that's where things go wrong. That's where people fall down.'

Cora walked into the room. She was carrying a bowl of fruit which contained blackened bananas, shrivelled oranges, and one bruised red apple. She put the fruit bowl down.

'Ah. The bullet whisperer's still here,' said Cora, picking up the apple and polishing it on her dress.

'Fuck off,' said Ken.

She pushed one of the horse brasses on a ceiling beam. Ken tutted and returned to testing bullets.

'Want a coffee?' asked Tom.

She nodded and he poured out coffee for them both. She sat down on a stool, stirred milk into her coffee and tapped the spoon on the rim of the cup. 'Want some fruit? The bananas are better than they look.'

'They look fucking ancient,' said Ken.

'Not asking you, am I?' said Cora, wandering over to the fireplace. She dropped two logs on to the embers and pushed the wood around with a brass poker until the flames started to catch. She put the fireguard on the hearth and walked back to the table.

'Anyway. What are you doing up before midday?' asked Ken.

Cora gave him the finger and said, 'I fancied some lunch. Tom? Lunch?'

'Wouldn't say no.'

'There's soup,' said Ken. 'Mulligatawny's good for weather like this.'

'What's that?' asked Tom.

'Mulligatawny. It's a soup,' replied Ken.

'I mean, what does it taste like?'

'Like a shit curry,' said Cora. 'I wouldn't bother.'

Cora sat down and pointed over at the bar. 'Tom. See where the chopping board is? For the lemons? Should be a small knife next to it.'

Tom saw a small fruit knife with a bone handle. 'This one?'

'That's the fella. Bring it over here.' Cora sorted through the fruit bowl.

Tom handed the knife to Cora. She cut the apple into quarters. One of the segments was black. She set it aside and said, 'Someone got scurvy up here once. Had to send him to hospital. His gums were all fucked up. Teeth falling out. The whole thing.'

'My nan used to warn us about scurvy,' said Tom. 'Her way of making us eat cauliflower.'

'Did it work?'

'Well. I never got scurvy.'

'This guy did,' she said. 'He never came back. Probably died.'

'You can't die from scurvy,' said Ken.

'Who told you that?'

'Frank.'

'Probably not true then, is it?' She picked up an orange, placed it on the table and, pressing lightly down with the palm of her hand, rolled it back and forth on the table. She peeled it carefully.

'If you're hungry,' said Ken, 'we're having pies for dinner when Frank gets back at five. Steak.'

'Not really steak, is it, Ken?'

'Yeah it fucking is.'

Cora lowered her voice. 'Do you want my advice, Tom?'

'Go on.'

'Don't bother,' she said.

'Fuck off, Cora,' said Ken.

'He gets offended by the way I talk about his pies. He's very protective of them. Aren't you, Ken?'

'They're good pies,' said Ken.

'You know how much he pays for those things?'

Tom smiled. 'Nope.'

'Go on. Take a wild guess.'

'I dunno. A pound a pie?'

'A quid? That's in the luxury range. No. Try again.'

'50p?'

'10p a fucking pie.'

'It's a bloody good deal,' said Ken.

'That's not even lips and arseholes,' said Cora. 'So. My advice? Have a piece of fruit. Tastes good. Keeps you regular. Right, Ken?'

'Fuck off.'

Cora laughed. 'Actually Tom, do you like bananas?'

'Yeah.'

'You know you can ask bananas questions?' she asked. 'Has to be a yes or no question. Bananas aren't that chatty.'

'Okay.'

She held the banana up to Tom like a microphone. 'Go on. Ask it a question.'

'Um. Okay.' He glanced at Ken. 'Is Ken going to fall over in the next five minutes?'

Cora cut off the bottom of the banana. 'See. What you do is you look in the middle. If you see a "y" then it's yes. If you see a dot, then it's no. Okay?'

'Right.'

'So. Is Ken going to fall over in the next five minutes?' Cora showed the cut end of the banana to Tom.

He squinted and drew in his breath. 'Bad news, Ken.'

'What?' asked Ken.

'Really bad news,' said Tom.

'Fuck off,' said Ken. 'The both of you.'

'Sorry, Ken,' said Cora. 'The banana never lies.'

Ken accidentally jogged the table. The two boxes of ammunition tipped over and the bullets rolled on to the carpet. Ken groaned and pulled at the knees of his trousers, knelt down, scooped up the bullets, and threw them into the 'unchecked' box. He put the boxes under his arms, and stalked off to the office.

Tom peeled the banana. Its mottled skin resembled brushed leather.

'Maybe I should go and see if he's okay,' said Tom.

'No. Don't. Really. Leave him.'

'Come on. Ken's had a hard time. He had to wash my pants.'

'You ever thought Ken might be playing this up a bit?'

'Ken? I'm not sure.'

'I bet you he not only falls over in the next five minutes but he does it in the next room just so we can hear it. 10p it happens. Or a pie. Your choice.'

'You're on.' Tom shook Cora's hand. She did not let go and turned his hand over and looked at his palms. The cracked and blistered skin.

'Do they hurt?' she asked.

'A bit.'

'Here. Put some of this on.'

She reached into her handbag and pulled out a small tube of moisturiser cream. 'Honestly. This stuff will help. '

'Will it?'

She smiled. 'Don't worry. I won't tell anyone.'

Tom applied some of the cream to his hands. He could smell oranges.

They talked for a long time and did not notice that the fire had nearly gone out. Tom went outside to chop more wood. A cold rain fell hard against the gravel. Large brown puddles had formed in the potholed yard. Tom lifted the tarpaulin from the woodpile. He selected a few knotted branches. Silver birch and beech. The bark was nearly grey. Lichen flaked away in his hands. He chopped the wood and gathered it up. The rain turned to sleet.

Tom returned indoors and placed one of the freshly cut logs on to the fire. The wood crackled and hissed and slowly blackened in the flames.

'You want a drink of something?' he asked.

'Should be some blackcurrant there?'

He bent down and searched the shelves and moved a small cardboard box. Underneath there were curled up bodies of woodlice, all hardened into little black ball-bearings. He reached to the back of the shelf and brought out two bottles. One contained turpentine, the other blackcurrant cordial.

'How strong do you like it?'

'Weak,' she said.

'Ice?'

'Won't be any.'

He poured out a measure of the cordial and filled up the glass with water.

'Can you see a bowl there?'

Tom saw a white ramekin next to the beer taps. 'This?'

'Perfect.'

He handed her the ramekin and the glass of juice.

She sipped at the drink and said, 'Blimey. Granny strength.'

The wind blew. Sleet fell from the grey clouds. Cora fiddled with the orange peel on the table and looked outside. She tapped the ash of her cigarette into the ramekin, and ran her fingers over the chipped edges. 'Ken bought this when he went to Hebden Bridge. Frank gave him a hundred quid. He was supposed to buy plates and cutlery. But he bought balloon whisks. And these things.'

'What did he get them for?'

'Cheese soufflés. He was bored and wanted to try something different. And you know what? They were amazing. Best thing I've eaten up here. Problem was he didn't know Frank hates cheese and anything that isn't a meat pie.'

'Or hard-boiled eggs.'

'Exactly. So that was that.'

Tom looked towards the back room. 'Has Ken fallen over yet?'

'Don't think so. But there's still time,' she said, putting down the ramekin. 'Frank will be back soon. He'll probably still be in a shit mood.'

'Why were they bringing in all that stuff yesterday?'

'What stuff?'

'Toolboxes. Paint. They put it in that room near my bedroom.'

'Fuck knows. Not good if they're planning to go in there though. It's sound-proofed,' she said.

Over the wind and sleet, they heard the distant roar of an engine. Cora lowered her head and exhaled.

'It's Frank. Keep your head down.'

CHAPTER TEN

S LEET WAS COMING down hard. Tom saw the truck
pull into the carpark. The engine stopped and the three
men climbed out. Braudy's overalls were spattered with dirt.
He wore yellow ear defenders and held a picnic hamper in
his arms. Tucker stalked off to the store carrying two shovels
and a pick axe.

Frank wore a raincoat over a pinstripe suit. Muddy
plastic bags covered his brogues. He shouted something at
Braudy, and ran towards the entrance, trying not to step in
the puddles. The front door opened. The pith and pieces of
orange peel stirred on the table. Frank marched in, took off
his sodden coat, and slung it over the back of a chair. There
was a smell of wet dog.

Frank stood there for a couple of seconds, looking at Tom
and Cora. 'You two been here all afternoon?'

'Just chatting,' said Cora. 'Passing the time.'

'Passing the time. Right.' He adjusted the lop-sided horse
brass on the beam, sat down on a stool, and pulled the plastic
bags off his feet. The front door opened. There was a sound
of shoes scraping on the doormat.

'Can I come in and get warm?' asked Braudy.

'You can come in when those shoes are off,' said Frank.

Braudy put down the picnic hamper and hung his ear
defenders on a coat hook.

'Is Ken about?' asked Frank.

'He was sorting bullets earlier,' replied Cora.

Frank took off one of his shoes and wrapped it in one of the plastic bags. He started on the other one, picking at the tightly knotted laces with his thumbnail.

'Can I come in now?' asked Braudy, picking up the picnic hamper.

'Go and wash up. And go and find out if Ken has our dinner ready.' Frank checked his watch. 'Check he's put on four pies. One extra for Tom.'

Braudy picked up the hamper and left the room

'Jesus,' said Frank. 'This fucking shoe.'

'Um. Frank? I might sit out dinner if that's okay,' said Tom.

'What?'

'I'm not that hungry.'

Cora touched Tom's toe with her foot. He looked at her.

'She been talking?' asked Frank. 'Cora? You been in his ear?'

'Tom's his own man,' she said.

'You'll eat with us, son. Not hungry. Bollocks. It's the best fucking pie in the north.'

Tom blew out his cheeks.

'Fuck off, Tom. Don't give me that fucking face. Big day tomorrow and before big fucking days, we eat. We get our heads straight.'

'I didn't even know I was helping tomorrow,' said Tom.

'You're helping all right, sunshine. Like you're eating. Okay?'

Tom glanced at Cora.

'Don't look at her. You look at me when I'm talking. Understand?'

'I didn't mean—'

'Don't fuck with tradition. Don't fuck with what's gone before. Right?'

Tom nodded.

'Pass me the box. White one on the counter.'

Tom handed the box over to Frank. Inside there was cutlery, a salt cellar, sachets of brown sauce. Frank took out a fork and used the tines to loosen the knots in his laces. The shoe slipped off and he wrapped it up in the other plastic bag. 'Right. Tom – lay out some knives and forks for us.'

'Okay.'

Braudy came out from the office. His hair was slicked back and he had changed into jeans and a Mark Knopfler T-shirt. His hands were scrubbed pink.

'Ken says pies ready in five minutes, Frank.'

Frank nodded and left the room. Braudy smirked and went behind the bar and poured himself a pint of bitter. Tom brought the box of cutlery over to the table. He laid out the knives and forks and set out the salt and the brown sauce.

'What did I say to you, Tom? About keeping your head down?' asked Cora.

'I was trying to be helpful.'

'You were being stupid.'

Tom sat down at the table and looked at the bag filled with Frank's muddy shoes. Outside, the wind had picked up. The sky was dark with storm clouds. The teddy bear tied to the front of the truck dripped with filthy water. Tucker came in cursing and unbuttoning his muddy overalls.

'Pint, mate?' asked Braudy.

'Heavy if there's any,' replied Tucker.

'Genius over there just pissed off Frank.'

'What you thinking, dickhead?'

The door to the office swung open. Frank walked in wearing a kimono and his old tartan slippers. He wandered over to the fire and threw on another log from the basket.

'Who chopped these?' he asked

'I did,' said Tom.

'Cut them smaller next time.' He moved over to Cora and planted a kiss on the top of her head. As he bent over, his kimono gaped. Tom caught a glimpse of dark, fleshy folds.

Frank clicked his fingers at Braudy. 'Get me a bottle from the fridge.'

'Which bottle?'

'Any.'

Tucker opened a bottle of stout and handed it to Frank. He took a swig and spilled a little on his kimono. 'Cora,' he said. 'Go upstairs. Wait for me there.'

'Now?' asked Cora.

'If you would.'

Cora picked up her bowl of fruit. She paused and handed a banana to Tom.

Frank watched her leave and then sat down. 'So, you hungry after all?'

'That's for afters,' said Tom.

'Fuck afters. Get one of them pies in your stomach. You won't need afters.'

'Here he comes,' said Braudy, taking a seat.

Frank looked at his watch and said, 'Five on the dot.'

Ken came in carrying a tray. He no longer wore the bobble hat. Only a faint outline of the penis drawn on his forehead remained.

Tom caught the heavy scent of sweaty onions. He felt

his throat tighten. Tucker stubbed out his cigarette and sat opposite Frank.

'Bruise looks better, Ken,' said Braudy.

'Does it?'

'Yeah. Less angry.'

Ken handed out the plates of food and left the room.

Tom looked at the pie. It was enormous and covered in peas and thick gravy. Frank opened up the pie with his fork, separated the pastry, and cut up the meat. Tucker and Braudy started to eat noisily.

'Get stuck in, Tom,' said Frank. 'While it's nice and hot. See any serviettes?'

Tom shook his head.

'I thought we had serviettes.' Frank shovelled some peas into his mouth.

'We've kitchen roll.'

'Fuck sake,' muttered Frank.

Tucker wiped gravy from his lips with the back of his hand. 'What's the timetable tomorrow?'

'We leave in the morning. Get to Oldham after lunch-time,' replied Frank, squirting a sachet of brown sauce over his boiled peas.

'Get out of here by ten?'

'What's the hurry, Tucker?' asked Frank.

'Good to get it over and done with,' said Tucker. 'Before the weather changes.'

Tom looked at his plate. The pie smelled like dog food. The small peas looked more grey than green.

'Think they'll be waiting for us?'

'Aye,' said Frank.

'We taking Tom?'

'Tom's got some things to do here with Ken.'

'What kind of things?' asked Tom.

'Eat your fucking tea,' said Frank.

Tucker pushed a piece of pastry around the plate, parting the gravy and leaving two white curves in its wake. 'When do we get back?'

'Four. Five. See what the weather does.' Frank pointed at Tom's plate. 'Problem, Tom?'

'No. No problem,' said Tom, quietly.

Frank put down his knife and fork. 'Are you listening to me?'

'Yes.'

'So why aren't you eating?'

Tom breathed out and cut into the pie with his knife. The pastry looked like cardboard left out in the rain. He prodded the coarse grey meat with his fork. His throat tightened again. He closed his eyes and placed the meat into his mouth. He bit down and heard a crunch. Gristle, bone. Tom could chew but could not swallow. He kept going, staring at the pie, which seemed to have grown larger. Braudy smiled. Tom cut a smaller piece, and put it in his mouth. He chewed slowly and tried to swallow. This time it caught in his throat. He choked. Tucker laughed.

Frank pushed his plate away in disgust. 'Fucking hell, Tom.'

Tom spat the meat on to his plate. He took out his handkerchief, wiped his eyes, and blew his nose. He shook his head and said, 'I'm sorry. I can't.'

'Most of your pie to go yet,' said Tucker.

Tom stared at him. 'Why don't you fucking have it?'

'See? She got to him, Frank. Pie's too good for her and all.'

Frank's expression hardened. 'Disappointing, Tom. Look at that. Feeble.'

'I'm sorry,' said Tom.

'Clear the table and get out of my sight.'

Tom rose slowly. The three men watched him as he picked up the plates.

'Tell Ken to come and see me,' said Frank. 'Need to leave someone in charge here tomorrow.'

Braudy laughed. 'Strength in depth, eh?'

'Aye. Tell me about it.'

Tom carried the plates through to the corridor and eased his way past the rolls of polythene. Ken was in the kitchen sitting at the table. He was reading the letters page of a pornographic magazine. There were dirty plates in the sink. The smell of the pies was still strong.

'Frank wants to see you,' said Tom.

Ken closed his magazine. 'Did you enjoy your pie?'

'I'm a bit off my food at the moment.'

Ken shook his head and closed the magazine. He left the room, whistling a Neil Diamond song to himself.

Eager for fresh air, Tom went over to the grease-covered window and tried to push it open. He couldn't. It was nailed shut. He scraped the remains of the pies and peas from the plate into a blue pedal bin. He opened the cupboard and, after a brief search, found the washing-up liquid. A dead mouse was curled up next to the bottle. Its black eyes were wide open. Tom carefully picked up the small body, and dropped it in the bin. He washed each plate, holding it to the light to make sure it was clear of gravy stains. He stacked the plates on the draining board, and sat at the table. The three women posing on the cover of Ken's magazine looked at him. He turned it over and listened to the groans made by the boiler mounted on the far wall.

Ken came in, pulling on a sweater. 'Frank wants to see you, Tom.'

'Now?'

'Upstairs.' Ken got a glass of water and sat down at the table. He squeezed out some of the cold sore remedy on to his finger and rubbed it on to his bottom lip.

'What is that stuff?'

'Lemon balm.' Ken pursed his lips. 'Tastes funny but it works.'

'I'll bear that in mind.'

'Pass me some socks. From the fridge.'

Tom picked out a woollen pair. They were bright green and soft. He handed them to Ken and looked at the single yoghurt pot. It had gone out of date the year before.

'Should I throw this away?'

'Don't fucking touch it,' said Ken, sitting down at the table. He took off his shoes and gave the green socks a careful sniff before he put them on.

'Better?'

'I wouldn't keep Frank waiting if I were you,' said Ken.

Tom reached the main office and tried a couple of the doors, and found the one that led through to a stairway. Spotlights shone down on the paisley wallpaper and pink carpet. He climbed the stairs and reached a wide landing. There were several doors, all closed. One of the doors was white and covered in old football stickers. Paintings hung on the walls. Landscapes of trees and winding rivers. Pale full moons partially hidden by mountains. Winter scenes. Summer scenes. There were initials in the corner of each painting. 'M. R. G.'

An old chest of drawers, missing one of its legs, was pushed up against a bricked-up window. There was a small, empty magazine rack on top of the drawers. Tom heard the hiss of water. Discordant whistling.

'Frank? Cora?'

The sound of water stopped but the whistling continued. Tom heard the flap of a towel and a door opened. Frank, naked, stepped out and Tom caught sight of Frank's bulging stomach which hung low against his grey cock and balls.

Tom turned away and shielded his eyes. 'Jesus. Sorry, Frank.'

'What's up, Tom?'

'I can come back in a minute.'

'Nah. We can talk now.' Frank rubbed the towel over his legs. 'Everything okay?'

'I ruined your meal.'

'Ah. It was just tea, Tom. Just a fucking pie, wasn't it?' Frank dried his chest. 'Tomorrow's getting to me a bit.'

'I know.'

'Tell me honestly. Is it them two? Braudy and Tucker? Or is it me?'

'Those two.'

'Bit rough on you back there. Just hard, you know? The fucking weather, dealing with Tucker and Braudy. Then coming back with my shoes full of water and seeing you with her.'

Tom held up his hand. 'No, Frank. No.'

'I know it was nothing. You were just talking.' He lifted one of his legs and wiped under his feet. 'Having a younger girlfriend. I don't know if Stephanie—'

'She was older.'

'Right. And that's hard enough, right?'

'It could be.'

'Moody sort.'

'Sensitive,' said Tom.

'Bookish. Highly strung.'

'What did you want to see me about?'

Frank wrapped the towel around his waist. 'Let's concentrate on tomorrow.'

Tom breathed out. 'Yeah.'

'Ken knows what to do. It's just a bit of moving around. A bit of prep.'

'Fine.'

'It'll be a long day, but it'll be better than this one. Has to be, doesn't it?'

CHAPTER ELEVEN

TOM WOKE UP and could smell drains. The bath, crusted with scum and dirt, made a gurgling sound. He heard something scratching on the inside of the walls. Unable to get back to sleep, he went across the corridor to the toilet. The pull switch was still broken, so he pissed in the darkness. Hoping his aim was true.

Tom picked out his warmest clothes, and put them on the silk-covered chair. He laid out his meat-smelling towel and turned on the bath taps. Steam from the bath flicked at the loose corners of newspaper pasted on to the wall. It took a minute before the water ran clear. Tom put the bath plug in and undressed. Hairs and dirt floated around on the surface of the rising water. He climbed into the bath when it was a third full. He turned off the taps and lay back. He looked at his arms. The veins and sinews. He thought of Stephanie and how he missed her. The water was very hot and, after a few minutes, he felt faint. He carefully got out and steadied himself against the side of the tub. He lay on the bed with the towel beneath him. He saw the dirty ceiling and things went black for a moment. He came to and covered himself with the towel. He went over to the bath and pulled out the plug. The scummy water gurgled as it drained away.

He got dressed, left his room, and stood in the corridor. It shared the damp silence of dilapidated churches. The kitchen lights were on.

'You there, Ken?'

He heard only the lights, the fridges. The room was cold and strip lights cast double shadows across orange linoleum. Sitting on the work surface was a baking tray containing leathery strips of bacon and broken pieces of black pudding. A few plates, greasy with brown sauce and congealed egg, rested in the sink. He ran the water and heard the boiler wheeze, and then fall silent. The water from the tap ran cold. Tom looked closely at the boiler. He pressed a couple of buttons. Nothing happened. He left the kitchen to go and find Ken. In the corridor, the rolls of polythene had been moved. The metal door was open and he peered inside. The white ceiling and walls were layered in plastic. A pale blue shower curtain hung from the ceiling and partially concealed a chair set in the middle of the room. In the corner, the paint cans and kettles sat on top of a trestle table.

Tom made his way through to the office. He listened for a few moments and heard the ticking of cooling radiators. On a desk, an angle-poised lamp illuminated a magazine. A girl called Sarah beamed from the wrinkled page. She had lifted up her gingham dress to look at her crotch. In her excitement, she had not noticed the blurry figure standing behind her.

The lights were on in the bar. The fire was low. There was a plastic toolbox sitting on the pool table. It contained pliers, hacksaws, hammers. He went to the front window and peered outside. Small flakes of snow fell and settled on icy puddles. The truck had gone. He went behind the bar and took one of the postcards off the cork board. It was from Mandy. She spoke of lagoons and sight-seeing. The hot weather, the pleasant patio bar. Frank, she wrote, hated it all.

Tom got a cup of coffee from the machine. He called out

again and heard no reply. Certain he was on his own, he walked behind the bar, picked up the phone, and dialled Gary's number. It rang twice before it was answered.

'Gary?'

'Who's this?' An unfamiliar voice.

'Is Gary there?'

There was a long pause followed by muffled sounds.

He heard breathing on the other end of the phone.

'Hello? Is Gary there?'

'It's Tom, isn't it?'

The line crackled. He thought he heard laughter.

'I'm looking for Gary. Can you put him on?'

'No.'

'Tell him it's Tom.'

Another crackle. Then silence. Tom hung up and heard a noise. The back door was slammed shut. Ken wandered in, dressed in a thick parka, trousers, bright blue wellingtons. A deerstalker. He took off his gloves and put his hat on the pool table. He slipped off his coat and threw it next to the toolbox. 'You eat those leftovers?'

'Was I supposed to?'

'They'll only go in the bin.'

Tom touched the radiator opposite the fireplace. 'The boiler was making funny sounds.'

'What kind of sound?'

'Crunching.'

'Did it make a choking sound?'

'Choking?'

'Yeah,' he said. 'Like a cough.'

'No. I don't think so.'

Ken took a scrap of paper from his pocket and flattened it

on the counter. He found a green biro next to the small stack of cups by the coffee machine. 'Here. Right. Let's see. Sound the oil tanks. Done.'

'I sounded it the other day.'

'Your reading didn't make sense.'

'Twenty inches?'

'You wrote down two inches. Daft cunt.'

'I wrote twenty.'

'Want me to show you the book?'

'What is it now?'

'Nineteen.' He went back to his list. 'Right. Plastic. Done. Shower curtain. Done.'

'When does Frank get back?'

The snow was getting worse. Ken glanced out of the window and said, 'Tucker was keen to get it done today. Of all days.'

'Couldn't they wait?'

'That's what I fucking said. And that twat Tucker tells me I'm behaving like some fucking old woman.'

There was a gentle tap at the door from the office. Cora poked her head around the corner. 'Water's off, Ken.'

'Give me twenty minutes.'

'Twenty minutes?'

'Give or take.'

She sighed. Underneath her thick dressing gown, she wore dark pyjamas patterned with hippos and lions. Her hair was up in a ponytail.

Ken rubbed his face and folded up the list. 'Right. The boiler.'

Cora sat at the bar. She took the cellophane off a packet of cigarettes and looked outside. With little more than a

whisper, the snow had already started to transform the l
andscape.

'They're not bloody getting back today, are they?' she said.

'Pick up that toolbox for us, Tom.'

Holding the box with two hands, Tom followed Ken into the office. Ken touched the radiator, shook his head, and carried on down the corridor.

'Boiler always struggles with weather like this. Should have checked it earlier.'

They reached the kitchen and Tom set the toolbox down on the floor. Ken took the cover off the boiler. He pushed a button and waited. He pushed the button again.

'Bollocks.' Ken pulled out a wrench from the toolbox. 'Switch off the stopcock. Cupboard under the sink.'

Tom opened the cupboard and moved out the bottles of bleach, the white vinegar, the bicarbonate of soda. Damp blue cloths and greasy rubber gloves. He reached back to a plywood panel and moved it out of the way to reveal the tap. He switched it off and ran the water until the flow dwindled to a trickle.

Ken turned a valve on the side of the boiler. There was a hiss and a clunk. He unscrewed something else and then picked out a screwdriver from the toolbox.

'I think I smell gas,' said Tom.

'How can you smell gas? This uses fucking oil, you tit.'

Tom sniffed the air again. 'It smells like gas.'

'Why don't you eat something and shut up?'

'The leftovers?'

'Yes, the bloody leftovers.'

Tom moved over to the table and took a piece of black pudding off the baking tray.

'Straight from the farm,' said Ken. 'Made the old way.'

There was a shout and Tom turned to see Cora walking quickly down the corridor.

'I said twenty minutes, Cora,' said Ken. 'You've given me two.'

'Someone's here.'

'What do you mean?'

'They're parking up outside.'

Ken looked over his shoulder. 'Is it Frank?'

'Someone else.'

'Tourists, then.'

'It doesn't look like a tourist.'

'Jesus. Okay. Tom, go and tell them we're closed.' He reached over and twisted another valve. There was a metallic click. 'Odd.'

'What?' asked Tom.

'Look. Go and see who it is,' he said. 'I'll catch up once I've fixed this.'

Tom and Cora left the kitchen. They entered the office and heard the hiss of static coming from the bar. Tom opened the door a crack and saw a man in a boiler suit. He was standing by the television, fiddling with the aerial. The white noise unchanging. He switched it off, sat down, and spread out a newspaper on the counter.

'Know him?' asked Tom.

'Can't see him properly. What's he doing?'

'Reading.' Tom closed the door. 'What do we do?'

'Wait until he gets bored,' she said. 'He'll go away after a while.'

'It's snowing. We'll be stuck with him.'

Tom pushed open the door again. The man chuckled to

himself, picked up his paper, and said, 'Stop with the games. I know you're both there.'

Tom closed the door.

'Look. I'll go,' said Cora.

'In your pyjamas?'

'What's wrong with them?'

They heard the man chuckle again.

'I'm waiting,' said the man.

Tom walked into the bar. The man held up the newspaper and folded it square. He sniffed and shook his head. 'Depressing to read. A once proud club, reduced to this. Begging for alms. Penury.' He held up the back page and pointed to the main photo. A Leeds United player. Exhausted, defeated, head bowed.

'You have to go. We're closed.'

The paper was lowered. The man had a crew cut. White crooked teeth. 'Galloway?'

'That's the one, Tom. That's me.' He took a sip of coffee.

'You passing through?'

'No, no. Not exactly.' He drummed his fingers quickly and took a cigarette stub from the ashtray. There was lipstick on the filter. He sniffed it and touched the tip. 'Cora was looking out of the window when I pulled up. Nice bit of trim, isn't she? Wasted out here.'

'You should leave.'

'Had a go on her, Tom?' he asked.

'What?'

'Had a go on her? Had a sniff?'

'Please go.'

Galloway put the newspaper down on the counter. His fingers were black from newsprint. He chuckled again and shook his head. 'I'm not going. Not yet.'

'What about the snow?'

Galloway looked out of the window. 'Always fun to do a bit of driving in the snow.'

Tom shifted weight from one foot to the other. 'Look, Galloway. I can offer you a drink, but you need to go afterwards.'

'Didn't come here for the mint juleps, Tom.'

'Then you need to go. We're closed.'

Galloway pulled out a gun. It looked like something from an old war movie. He pointed it at Tom. He pulled up a stool and patted the cushion.

Tom licked his lips and sat down. 'You know Frank will be back. Soon.'

Galloway looked at his watch. 'He's not back until four. At least.'

'He phoned about an hour ago,' said Tom. 'Said he'd be home earlier.'

'Good try, Tom. Good try. No. I have it on very good authority that Frank won't be back until at least four. Later, if this snow carries on.'

A low metallic hum filled the room. Hidden pipes rattled and vibrated before settling on a deep resonant note. There was a splash and gurgle from the radiators. Galloway reached into his coat pocket and took out a photograph. It had been folded and a white crease ran down through the centre of the image. Galloway looked at it and Tom could see the blue heart drawn in biro on the reverse side.

'This here is a picture of Stephanie Conway. Recognise it?'

'Yes.'

'Good-looking girl. Shame what happened to her. Dying like that. Word is that it's your fault.' Galloway put the photograph away. 'Worked in the museum, didn't she? Coins. Roman pots. Swords. Buried junk.'

'How did you know that?'

'You can find out a lot when you know who to ask.'

'Tell me why you're here.'

He took a deep breath and said, 'Couple of days ago, Stephanie's family raised the price on your head. You know that? About the price?'

Tom shrugged.

Galloway put his hands on the counter. He shook his head and said, 'You must have done something terrible for them to want you this badly.'

'I didn't do anything.'

'Aye. Well her family seem to think you not doing anything was the fucking problem.'

'You don't know what happened.'

'Me? I don't give a shit. You can plead your case with her old man. Or the dead daughter ombudsman. Whatever. All I know is that Conway's willing to hand over a quarter of a million quid to bring you in alive. Fifty thousand if you're dead.'

'I'm not coming with you.'

'You bloody well are,' he said, cocking the gun.

'What if I run?'

'Nothing to say I can't hand you over injured. Besides, fifty thousand isn't too bad either. Up to you.'

The snow pattered against the window. A gust of wind made the fire gutter.

Galloway sighed. 'You got a coat?'

'In my room.'

'And where's your room?'

'Back there.'

'Fuck it. Your jumper will see you right. Come on. Get on the floor.'

Tom got down on his knees. He felt sick. His mouth was dry. Galloway lowered the gun and pushed him to the ground. The carpet smelled of vinegar and stale beer.

'Hands behind your back.'

Tom felt handcuffs close around his wrists.

'Those too tight?'

'No.'

The door at the back opened. Ken peeked through. 'Is that you, Galloway?'

Galloway leaned close to Tom and whispered, 'Say anything and I'll kill him. Blood will be on your hands. Okay?'

Tom nodded.

'Morning, Ken. Thought you'd be out making snowmen,' said Galloway.

'I was fixing the boiler.'

'Take it slow, Tom. Left leg first. There.'

'What's this about, Galloway?'

'Now the right leg. Up you get.'

Tom got to his feet. Galloway gripped his arms tight.

'Did Frank know you were coming?' asked Ken.

'Nothing to worry about.' The gun jabbed into Tom's ribs. 'That right, Tom?'

He nodded.

'Louder. So Ken can hear.'

'Yeah.'

'See? Nothing to worry about. I'm happy. Tom's happy. You go back to your boiler.'

'I fixed it.'

'Well, go back to it anyway. Give it a bit of a polish. We're good here. Aren't we, Tom?'

'Frank didn't say anything about you coming here,' said Ken.

'Old Frank's getting on a bit. Maybe it slipped his mind.'

Ken shook his head. 'This isn't right.'

Galloway's smile faded. He lifted his gun and pointed it at Ken. 'You're holding me and Tom up now. We've got a drive back. So let's have your hands up. Good. Now. Turn around.'

'Galloway—'

'Be a good boy now. Turn around.'

Ken turned. His gun was tucked into the waistband of his trousers.

'Throw that over here.'

Ken tossed the gun over. It clattered at Galloway's feet. He reached down and put it in his jacket pocket. 'Anything else I need to know, Ken?

'No.'

'Good. Get on the floor. Face down.'

'But—'

Galloway pushed the gun up against Tom's nose. 'Help me out here. Ken's not listening.'

Tom swallowed.

'Tell him, Tom.'

'Lie down.'

'Louder.'

With a sudden movement Tom took a bite at Galloway's wrist. His teeth pinched at muscle and tendon. He bit down hard. Galloway gasped and then shrieked. The gun went off. The bullet hit the television, smashing the screen dead centre.

Tom bit down again. This time, Galloway dropped his

gun, and the two men fell backwards. They hit the trophy shelf and smashed it. Frank's golf and darts trophies fell to the floor and the plastic figures snapped off. Tom felt the dart trophy jabbing into his back. He bit down harder on Galloway's wrist and felt long fingers claw and probe at his nostrils and his eye sockets. He saw Galloway's face. The wild eyes. A twisted mouth. Lips formed into something between a smile and grimace. Revealing his white, uneven teeth. And then something happened to them. Black blood, flowing. Tom turned to see Cora brandishing a club hammer, smashing it into Galloway's face again and again. His smile was slowly beaten back. Blood splashed on the carpet. Cora kept hitting him until Galloway's body become heavy and limp. Tom relaxed his jaws and released Galloway's bloody wrist. He lay there for a few moments and tried to ask Cora if she was okay. The words would not come. Ken stood beguiled by the bloodied thing lying before him.

Tom got up from the floor and Cora picked up some kitchen paper. She wiped the blood from his lips.

'The handcuffs,' he said.

Ken hesitated. 'Is he dead?'

'Still breathing.'

Ken knelt down, searched through Galloway's pockets and found the keys. He handed them over to Cora and she unlocked the handcuffs. Tom sat down on a stool, touching his wrists where the cuffs had bitten into the skin. His jumper was torn. His skin was grazed. The three of them looked at Galloway. He was still smiling.

CHAPTER TWELVE

T OM PISSED IN the steel urinal. He looked at the
photograph hanging on the wall. The woman's hands
were slightly blurred. Movement from when the photo had
been exposed. It gave the picture a sense of life. He wasn't
sure if he liked it or not.

He went to wash his hands. The lights flickered briefly.
He could still taste blood, so rinsed out his mouth again. His
spit was red-orange. He checked his bruises in the mirror and
went back to the bar. The bright lights made him feel sick. The
ceiling seemed too low and the dark carpet, the white walls,
were strangely oppressive. Over in the corner, Galloway was
handcuffed to a radiator. He was laid out on three turquoise
towels they had put down to protect the carpet. His mouth
and wrist were bloodied and bruised. There was a sharp smell
of urine.

Ken was staring down at the counter. Deep in thought. He
noticed Tom and nodded at him.

'When did Cora go up?' asked Tom.

'Five minutes ago. Have a beer.'

Tom threw a log on to the fire and then got a cold bottle
of beer from the fridge. He held it against his bruises until
the stinging eased.

'Try the phone,' said Ken.

Tom picked up the receiver. There was no dial tone.

'Any better?'

'A bit,' said Tom.

'It'll pass. You'll have some nice bruises to show off.'

Snow was still falling outside. Tom looked down at the broken trophy shelf. It had snapped in two. Ken had gathered up the little plastic men and placed them on one of the tables. 'Here. Tom. Pass me Galloway's gun. Over there. By his coat.'

Tom weighed Galloway's gun in his hand. 'Is this a Luger?'

'Give me that.'

He handed the gun to Ken, who put his cup down, and sat at the bar. He pushed the bullets out on to the counter. Tom picked one up and held it up to the light. The tip of the bullet had a cross cut into it.

'7.65mm parabellum,' said Ken. He shook one of the bullets near his ear and smiled. 'Have a listen.'

'What?'

'It's a dud.'

Tom nodded towards the smashed television. 'Looked dangerous enough to me.'

'Old ammunition goes off. Just not all the time.'

'Right.'

'It's about reliability.' Ken picked up another bullet and tested it. 'Dud.'

'Do you think Wayne will send anyone up here to look for Galloway?'

'Too early to say.'

'But he might?'

'Don't worry about that for now.'

Ken put the bullets in his pocket. He knelt down by Galloway and checked he was still breathing. 'We should get him out of here before he wakes up.'

'Maybe we should wait for Frank,' said Tom.

'Not worth the risk. Safe room should do for now. Come on. Let's get it over with.' Ken reached down, unlocked the handcuffs, and lifted Galloway by his left leg. Tom took Galloway's other leg.

'One. Two. Three.'

With a heave, they pulled Galloway across the carpet. He looked around in dazed wonder. His words were slurred by his swollen tongue and broken teeth. They dragged him through to the back office. They stopped. Ken was wheezing and sat against one of the workbenches to catch his breath. Galloway was trying to speak. He was asking for help. Begging for mercy.

They reached the safe room. Tom turned on the lights. Ken dragged Galloway into the room. There was a faint static crackle as Galloway's boiler suit rubbed against the plastic sheeting.

Ken kicked him hard in the ribs and went over to one of the toolboxes. He took out a length of nylon rope, planted a knee in the small of Galloway's back, and tied up his feet and hands. Then he took the other end of the rope, tied a slipknot, and looped the noose around Galloway's throat. As he struggled, the noose tightened. Ken wiped his nose with the back of his hand and said, 'Come on. We'll leave him.'

They both left the room and Ken locked the door with a brass key. His hands were splashed with blood. The lights flickered again. Tom looked up and saw lightbulbs hanging from twisted white cables. A draught caused them to swing gently.

They returned to the bar. Ken folded up the bloodied turquoise towels and put them on the pool table. Tom looked at his reflection in the window. The bruises had darkened around his cheeks and his eyes.

Ken came over and sat near him. 'My fucking feet. I ask you.'

'Hurting?'

'Stinging.' He took off his shoes and socks. His dirty toes were swollen and red.

Tom searched Galloway's coat. He found mints and hand cream. Lint, loose change. He emptied another pocket, and found the photograph of Stephanie. He looked at the picture. It was covered in finger prints and the colours had started to fade. He tried to remember the day he had taken the picture. The springtime warmth. The terracotta rooftops, the cool blue of sky and sea. It was like it had all happened to someone else. Ken took the photo off Tom. He looked at it. 'What's he doing with this?'

'Tucker gave it to him. The other night.'

Ken handed the photo back and slumped back in his chair, shaking his head in disgust. Tom looked at Galloway's car parked outside. Dirty snow had drifted up against its side.

'We need to move his car. Make sure no-one can see it from the road,' said Ken.

'Where?'

'Put it around the back. Chuck some tarpaulin over it. Snow will do the rest.'

'Where's the tarp?' he asked.

'The store. Take my coat and gloves.'

'Are you not coming?'

'One man job,' said Ken. 'Off you go.'

Tom put on Ken's gloves and coat. He took Galloway's car keys and pressed the remote to unlock the doors. The car beeped and blinked dimly through a layer of fallen snow. He stepped into the yard and pulled up his hood. The security light came on.

He approached Galloway's car and cleared the windscreen with his arm. He climbed into the car and turned the ignition. The dashboard lit up and the stereo came on. It was Fleetwood Mac. Tom wasn't sure which album. He switched off the music and drove the car to the back of the yard and parked it next to the fishing boat.

Tom got out of the car and walked over to the storage shed. He opened the door and stepped inside. He could smell oil and paint. Damp wood. Water dripped on to one of the workbenches. He saw a sheet of dark green tarpaulin sitting next to the stripped engine of a diesel lawnmower. He lifted up the tarp and left the store. The breeze had picked up and the snow stung Tom's face. He unfurled the tarp over the car and weighed down the corners with a few bricks and a gas canister.

Back in the Bothy he kicked snow from his shoes and took them off. He hung up the coat and took off his gloves. Ken was sitting at the bar drinking whisky and eating cheese and chive crisps.

'Is the snow thick?' he asked.

'Two inches.'

Ken tipped the remaining crisps into his mouth and licked his fingers. 'Looked like a nice motor, that. Good to drive?'

'I guess.'

'Roomy, I bet. Lots of power.'

Tom sat near the window and rubbed his hands together. He looked down at his feet and saw spots of blood on the carpet where Galloway had fallen.

'Did you tie down the tarpaulin?' asked Ken.

'Weighed it down with bricks.'

'Bricks? That all?'

'Yeah,' said Tom.

'You didn't secure it with rope?'

'Didn't see any rope.'

'The tarp will blow away without rope. Bricks won't do it. Not in weather like this.'

'You're welcome to go and sort it out if you like, Ken.'

'Tarp's probably halfway to Sheffield by now.'

They opened a couple of bottles of beer and drank them in silence. Tom kept looking over his shoulder, sure someone else was waiting outside. Ken went to the kitchen and returned wearing a fresh pair of socks. He had a small tool kit with him, which he set down on the table. He clicked open the catches, and lifted the lid. Inside there were cans of spray and oil. Files, pipe-cleaners. A silk cloth. He took out his pistol from the waistband of his trousers, and released the magazine. Then he pulled back the slide, removed the barrel, and ran a silk tow through the shaft until it was clean.

Tom stood by the window. Snow continued to fall. He looked further west and saw the distant flash of headlights sweep across the landscape. 'Someone's coming.'

'Bollocks,' said Ken.

'There are headlights.'

Ken looked out. 'I don't see it.'

'There. It's not Wayne, is it?'

'Nah. Wayne would come the other way.'

They listened. Burning logs popped in the fire. Ken hiccuped. Over the wind, they heard the familiar roar of Frank's truck. A crunching gear change.

'Should have gritted the bloody yard,' said Ken. 'Did you see any? In the store? Near the trellis panels?'

'Grit? No.'

They watched Frank's truck move slowly along the road and drive into the yard. Frank got out of the truck. He wiped his feet and entered the Bothy. His cheeks were red and stiff from the cold. There was snow on his shoulders.

Braudy came in, shivering. His lips were nearly blue and he wore ear defenders over a black beanie hat.

'Braudy. Get back out there,' said Frank. 'Sort out the fucking truck like I asked you to.'

'Can I get warm first?'

'You can get warm once you've checked the truck. Top up the antifreeze,' he said. 'Oil. All of that.'

'We're not going anywhere tonight, are we?'

'Just do it.'

Braudy nodded and went back out to the truck.

Frank hung up his cagoule. His jumper and jeans were soaking wet. 'Are the phones down?'

'Have been since it started snowing.'

'Fuck sake. We got stuck over on the moor. Braudy drove us into a fucking drift. Had to dig our way out.' He crossed over to the bar and saw the bloodied towels. He saw the broken trophies. The plastic figures. The hole in the television. He sniffed the air. 'What the fuck happened here?'

'We had a visitor. Galloway.'

Frank saw the bruises on Tom's face and neck.

'Where's Cora?'

'She's upstairs,' said Ken. 'A bit shaken.'

'But not hurt?'

'No.'

Tom looked out of the window. Braudy had lifted the bonnet and was pouring bright blue antifreeze into the radiator. Tucker stood next to him holding a torch. He rested a large bottle of engine oil on the carburettor.

Frank sat hunched in his chair. He picked wax from his ear and said, 'Get me a brandy, Ken.'

Ken picked up a stained pony glass from the shelf. 'Cognac? Or the Tesco stuff?'

'Tesco will do.'

'Tesco it is. Ice?'

'Just give me the fucking drink, Ken.'

Tom took out the photo of Stephanie and put it in front of Frank. 'Galloway had this with him.'

Frank picked up the picture and looked at it. He bit his thumbnail and swore under his breath. 'Is this the only copy?'

'Should be a blue heart on the back.'

Frank turned the picture over and nodded. 'Mind if I keep this for a little while?'

'Sure.'

Frank put the picture in his trouser pocket and stared out of the window.

Outside, Braudy slammed the bonnet shut, and took off his ear defenders. Tucker opened the driver's door and pulled out a large black sleeping bag from the back of the truck. It was heavy. The two men struggled to pull it across the yard. The bag moved. Something was inside it.

The front door opened and there was a gust of cold air. The sleeping bag was hauled into the middle of the room and Tucker kicked at it again. He smiled and then saw Tom standing by the pool table. He went pale.

Frank smiled broadly and slapped Tucker on the back. 'All okay?'

Tucker wiped at his mouth and gave a faint nod.

'Braudy. All finished?'

'Done the best I can.' He looked around the room, unnerved by the silence.

'Why don't you get yourself a drink?'

Braudy took the plaster off his right ear. He took out the cotton wool and sniffed it. He picked up a glass and went behind the bar. 'Anyone else want a pint?'

'You carry on,' said Frank.

'Who's in the bag?' asked Ken.

'Open it up, Tucker.'

Tucker crouched and unzipped the bag. Inside, there was an unconscious man. He had fuzzy hair and a soul patch. He had been badly beaten. The welts and wounds were raw. Frank knelt down and touched the man's face almost tenderly. 'We were wrong to bring him.'

Braudy put down his beer. 'Wrong?'

'We don't need him.'

'Hang on. We moved heaven and earth to get this fucker.'

'Don't need him,' said Frank. 'Finish your beer and take him out to the yard. Weigh down the bag. Cold will do the rest.'

'Want me to help?' asked Tucker.

'Oh no. Not you.' Frank held Tucker by the shoulders. 'You come with me for a chat. Tom. Ken. You come along too.'

The wind moaned outside. Tucker caught sight of the blood-stained towels on the pool table and looked over at Braudy who shrugged. Frank opened the door to the office.

Tucker and Ken went through. Tom followed them and closed the door behind him.

In the corner of the office, the angle-poise lamp shone brightly and cast shadows on the wall. Tom heard the building creak. There was another sound. Something pained and desperate. Tucker looked around at Frank, who smiled and pushed him forward. In the corridor, the sound grew louder as they approached the safe room. Ken took out his keys and unlocked the metal door.

Frank smiled. 'In you go, Tucker.'

Tucker entered the room and saw the hog-tied figure of Galloway lying on the floor. Blood was spattered on the plastic sheets. Galloway cried out and tried to crawl away into the corner. Ken kicked him hard in the testicles and stamped down on his ankle.

'Recognise him?' asked Frank.

Tucker shrugged.

Frank reached down and lifted Galloway's head. 'Come on, mate. Don't insult my fucking intelligence.'

Tucker nodded.

'Speak up,' said Frank.

'It's Galloway.'

Frank let go of Galloway's head. 'Funny he's up here, isn't it? Away from his friends.'

'Maybe he was just passing.'

'On a day like this? Bit fucking risky, isn't it? Knowing what'd happen if I saw him. After all the shit him and Wayne have put me through.'

'Frank—'

'Did you invite him up here?'

'No,' said Tucker.

'Sure?'

Unable to stomach Galloway's groans or the stink of his distress, Tom turned to leave. Frank pushed him up against the wall. 'You stay unless I say otherwise. Okay?'

Tom closed his eyes. Frank turned back to Tucker and gave him a menacing smile. Ken walked over to the trestle table and picked up one of the kettles. He filled it with water from the tap in the corner, and switched it on.

'Remember earlier? Over breakfast?' asked Frank. 'The bad weather. The ice. The threat of snow. I wanted to delay going. Didn't I? But you insisted we go. Remember that?'

Tucker tried to smile. 'Trying to do right by you.'

'Lucky for Galloway, wasn't it? You insisting us not being here.'

Tucker put his hands up. Palms out. 'I don't know anything.'

'Yeah. You do. But it's okay.' Frank glanced over at Galloway. 'We can always ask your mate what happened.'

'This is bullshit,' said Tucker.

The kettle started to hiss. Frank held up the photograph of Stephanie. Tucker put a shaking hand over one of his eyes so he could focus on the picture. His eyes flickered to the door. He licked his trembling lips.

'You told me you'd fucking burnt this.'

'It's a copy.'

Frank grabbed Tucker's hair and bounced his head off the side of the metal door, and then kicked at his knees. He fell to the floor and Frank picked him up again.

'You lied to me, you fucking cunt.'

Tucker looked up at Tom. 'You've got the wrong man, Frank.'

'Have I?'

Tom could hear the water in the kettle boil. Steam came out of the spout. Frank grabbed hold of Tucker and told Tom to stand back. Ken threw the boiling water at Tucker. It hit his chest and he screamed in pain and fell to the ground. Frank kicked him again and Ken filled the kettle up with more water.

Tucker clutched at his scalded chest and pointed at Tom. 'Him. It's him. Playing tricks on you. It was him who planted that picture on Galloway.'

Frank kicked him in the ribs and put his foot on Tucker's throat. He handed the photo back to Tom.

'We have a lot to talk about, sunshine,' said Frank, clicking his fingers. 'Tom. Ken. Bind him.'

Ken rummaged through the red toolbox. He pulled out a length of rope and said, 'Tom. Hold him down, there's a good lad.'

Tucker thrashed around. Frank kicked him in the head.

'Come on, Tom. Get stuck in. Hold him still.'

Tom knelt down quickly and held Tucker's legs while Ken tied them up. The metal door creaked open and Braudy stepped into the room. He looked at the two men lying on the floor. Tom got up quickly and left the room. The awful smell and the agonised cries followed him down the corridor.

CHAPTER THIRTEEN

Tom lay in the darkness listening to the sounds coming from the safe room. The bruises on his face ached. He got up and switched on the bath taps to drown out the noise. He buried his head under his pillow. It was not until dawn that the moans and shouts of suffering relented. He switched off the bath taps and got dressed. After making sure he had Stephanie's picture on him, he left his room, and went through to the bar.

All the lights were on. A single log smouldered in the fire. There was a smell of pencil shavings. The surface of the pool table was wet. He looked up and saw a dark stain on the ceiling. An iron bucket caught the water that dripped through the cracks in the plaster. The turquoise towels had been removed from the counter. A few bloodied pieces of kitchen paper had been screwed up and thrown into the bin.

Tom switched on the coffee machine and sat at the bar. He looked over towards the corner of the room and noticed the smashed television was no longer there. Only a tangle of wires remained. He went over to the wall and saw a bullet hole in the plaster.

Tom tried the phone. It was still dead. He stood at the front door. The cold air was sharp and a smell of rendered fat hung in the air. The snow had frozen overnight. Clinging to the underside of the eaves, a row of icicles shone brilliantly in the sunlight. Plump drops of water fell from the tips and landed rhythmically on the rotten woodwork. He looked up and saw black smoke rising into the clear sky.

After his coffee, he put on his shoes and crossed the yard. He saw the black sleeping bag was folded up outside the coal shed. He reached the woodpile and selected a mossy branch and picked up the axe. He checked it was sharp enough and rested the wood on the chopping block. He brought the axe down hard. It took four blows to cut through the trunk. He chopped the wood into foot-long segments, took the pieces back indoors, and threw them on to the fire. Then, he took the tape measure, the notebook of oil level measurements, and returned outside. He passed Galloway's car. The tarpaulin was covered in snow. He weighed down the corners with another couple of bricks and went around the back of the building past the caravans and the climbing frame. The smashed television sat in one of the skips amongst paint cans, bricks, and torn bin bags. He saw the mounds of rubbish and tried to imagine how the yard might smell during the summer.

The oil tank was topped with wet snow. He climbed up and took a reading. The level was at seventeen inches. He cleaned off the tape measure and wrote down the measurement in the notebook.

Back indoors, he warmed himself by the fire. It was past midday and he was hungry. In the corridor, pipes hummed, and water flowed. He walked past the safe room quickly and entered the kitchen. The only thing he could hear were the refrigerators and the boiler. He switched on the kettle and sat down at the table. The scratched surface was marked with coffee rings and dried smears of brown sauce. He picked up the old menu covers and stacked them on top of the old micro-wave. He wiped the table clean with a blue cloth. Then he looked for something he could eat. In one of the cupboards, he found a packet of dried noodles that had gone out of date the previous March. He boiled a little water, tipped in the noodles, and waited until they were soft and grey.

After he washed up his bowl, he walked past the safe room, trying to ignore the shouts. It was warm in the bar and the fire burned fiercely. Frank was standing by the window, smoking a cigarette. He held a creased handkerchief in his left hand.

'Coffee there,' said Frank.

'I've had some.'

'Have some more.'

Tom took the carafe from the machine and poured himself a cup. He saw Braudy was outside, clearing snow with a shovel.

'Braudy's wearing my gloves,' said Tom.

Frank blew his nose. 'Power cut again last night.'

'I didn't notice.'

'Did you sleep?'

'Yeah. A little.'

'No noise?'

'A bit.'

'That room's supposed to be soundproof. I have my doubts.'

For a little while, they watched Braudy slowly digging a shallow trench near the front wall. He was red faced and out of breath. He stopped and touched the base of his spine.

Frank put out his cigarette. 'Always too slow that one. Still thinks Tucker's innocent. Despite the evidence.'

'I don't know what I would say if it was my friend,' said Tom.

Frank took out his handkerchief and folded it over. Tom saw a red monogram stitched into the corner. 'F. L. G.'

Tom swirled the coffee grounds around in his cup.

'I have to thank you, Tom,' he said, 'for what you did. Takes a lot of courage to take on Galloway. You'd be dead by now. If he'd taken you back.'

'Don't think the Conways are people interested in quick deaths.'

Frank smiled at him and said, 'Stick with me, Tom. I'll make sure those cunts won't get near you.'

'Is Cora okay?'

Frank dabbed his forehead with the handkerchief and then wiped his nose. 'So stubborn, that girl. Like her father. She ever tell you about him?'

'No.'

'Headstrong. It's what got him in trouble.' Frank tapped his watch and listened to it. 'She went for a walk. Half an hour ago. In a bloody huff about something.'

'Want me to get her back?'

'You don't need to do that, Tom.'

'I don't mind.'

Frank watched the icicles outside the window. 'It'd save me a bit of bother,' he said.

'I know.'

Frank checked his watch again. 'I have more to do with Galloway and Tucker. And she's in a bad mood. You know how it is sometimes.'

Tom found a pair of red wellingtons in the lobby which were roughly his size. He put on the jacket Ken had worn the day before. A pair of mittens were stuffed into the pockets. He stepped outside into the icy breeze and looked up at black smoke rising from the chimney. A crow carrying a pebble in its beak hopped across the snow. It spread its wings and flew away.

Tom crossed the road and reached a fence. He climbed over it and followed Cora's footprints up the hill. When he reached the crest he stopped to catch his breath. He looked back at the Bothy. The snow concealed the joins between the mismatched extensions and adjuncts. Only the pall of black smoke blotted the scene. He turned, and saw Cora in the distance. She wore an orange coat and a bobble hat.

'Cora!'

The figure stopped, waved and then carried on. Tom started down the hill. After a few minutes he saw her stop, and walk back towards him. She had mirrored sunglasses on and a Manchester City scarf tied in a half-bow knot. They met up near an upturned trough and she smiled at him. Her cheeks were red and soft from the cold.

'It's very quiet, isn't it?' asked Tom.

'You out here for the day, or have you been sent out on an errand?'

'Frank wants you to come back.'

'So he can have a go at me again?'

'He's worried about you being out in the cold.'

'Speak for him and you'll end up speaking like him.'

Tom shielded his eyes from the bright sun. She took off a glove and put her hand under her armpit. He saw his reflection in her sunglasses.

'You got the picture back, then. Of Stephanie,' she said. 'Can I see it?'

Tom took the photo out and handed it to her. She lifted her sunglasses, looked at it, and then handed it back. The sun was high and bright. Although his feet were cold, his face felt warm. They carried on walking. They reached a low stone wall. Snow had drifted up against the side.

'She looks nice. What did she used to do?'

'She was a curator. Made displays and exhibitions.'

'Like what?'

'Lots of bullets and swords. Old tools. Roman stuff. Her parents hated her doing it. Thought she was wasting her time. Her dad used to shout at her about it. Reduce her to tears. Make her feel worthless.'

'What really happened to her, Tom?'

He sighed and took off his mittens. 'It happened three weeks ago. A car accident. I was driving. There was ice. We hit a tree.'

'Were you hurt?'

He didn't look at her and brushed some snow off the top of the wall.

'Her family said I didn't do enough to help her,' he said.

'You helped her out of the car though. You called an ambulance?'

Tom nodded.

'And you weren't drink driving or anything?'

'No.'

'None of this makes sense.'

'I answered your question, Cora.'

Cora frowned.

'I've had a shit time of it,' he said. 'From them. Her family. Their fucking mates. Calling me up and saying they're going to kill me. Sending me bullets in the post. Telling me I'd get lynched if I went to her funeral.'

'But it was a car accident.'

'They would have blamed me if she'd died from cancer.'

'Why do they hate you so much?'

Tom thought for a moment, and said, 'They've hated me since I wanted her to get help. Counselling.'

'Why didn't they want that?'

'They were afraid the law would get involved.' Tom looked at their footprints in the snow. They had taken an eccentric route. He could still see the column of black smoke rising over the crest of the hill. Whenever the wind blew he caught the scent of burning rubber.

'Maybe this is the safest place for me,' he said.

'People don't live long up here. They end up putting too much faith in Frank and stop looking after themselves.'

'What about you?'

'I'm here until Frank decides he's had enough of me.' She looked out at the white hills, the yellow horizon.

'Or until he dies.'

'Nah. If he dies, he'll take me with him.'

They turned and trudged back up the hill in silence. They stopped to take in the view. The distant outcrops of rock that reached up and clawed at the sky. A dark fringe of woodland.

Tom looked down at the Bothy. Braudy was still gritting in the yard. He was carrying a sack of grit on his shoulder. He dropped it down near the front wall and walked to the side of the building. He unzipped himself and pissed into the snow.

'Charming,' said Cora.

She started down the hill and Tom followed her. She helped him over the stone wall and they crossed the road. Near the store, Braudy threw down more grit on the cleared areas of snow, staining it a dull muddy brown. He took off Tom's gloves, and touched his infected ear. He wiped his hands on the side of his coat, and stared at them going into the Bothy.

Inside, they took off their coats, gloves and boots. Cora looked up at the low beam and pushed another horse brass askew. She sat near the fire, and Tom pulled up a chair.

'How long were Braudy and Tucker mates for?'

'Years,' said Cora. 'Used to thieve cars together in Leeds. Think they came up here about three years ago.'

'Only three?'

She draped her socks on the fireguard. 'Want to dry yours too?'

Tom took off his socks. The soles of his feet were dirty and he muttered an apology.

'Couldn't find a matching pair?'

'It's all that was clean,' said Tom, moving away from the fire.

Cora put the socks next to her own and moved the fireguard closer to the flames. Tom watched her pluck black lint from between her toes. The iron bucket under the leaking ceiling was nearly full.

Somewhere in the building, he heard a door slam. There was a shout. A squeak of hinges. Frank entered the room, wiping sweat from his brow. He was wearing black welding gloves and a heavy leather apron stained with white paint and blood. He went behind the bar, got himself a brandy, and knocked it back in one. He took off his gloves and threw them down on to the bar. 'Is Braudy still fucking gritting?'

'Yeah.'

'How long does it take?'

'There's a lot of snow,' replied Cora.

He wiped at his nose with a handkerchief. 'You pissed off with me?'

'I'm here, aren't I?'

'Go upstairs, Cora. Have a shower. Warm yourself up.'

'I'm happy enough here.'

'It's warmer upstairs. Go.'

She frowned and picked up her socks. Frank watched her leave the room. He lit a cigarette. He was quiet for a while. There were flecks of blood on the back of his neck and in his hair.

'How was she when you found her?' he asked.

'She was okay.'

'Did you talk to her about Galloway? About what happened?'

'No.'

Frank rubbed the back of his neck and looked at his clipped fingernails. 'Come on, Tom,' he said. 'Be level with me.'

'We didn't talk about it.'

'But you talked about me?'

'We didn't. I promise.'

Frank stubbed out his cigarette, and poured himself another brandy. 'Galloway told me about the price on your head. How much it is.'

'I don't care.'

'It's quarter of a million quid, Tom.'

'You sound impressed.'

'You should have said something.'

Tom looked at the fire and listened to the scrape of Braudy's shovel on the snow. He caught sight of water dripping from the ceiling. The plaster was loose. Crumbling.

'Galloway mentioned your friend. Greg.'

'Gary.'

'Sorry. Gary. Happened three or four days ago. Don't know what went on. Don't want to know if I'm honest. Wayne and his cunts.'

'Oh no.'

'Sorry I had to tell you.'

'He's gone?'

'Yes.' Frank looked at the horse brass Cora had moved. He reached up and set it straight. He patted Tom on the back and sat down next to him.

'Did Gary say anything to you?' asked Tom. 'When you spoke to him.'

'Spoke to him?'

'Few days ago. You said you'd spoken to him.'

Frank grimaced and touched the back of his neck. 'I owe you an apology, Tom.'

Tom rose from his seat.

'Sit yourself down, Tom. No need to make this into something it isn't.'

'You lied.'

'Please.' He pointed at the chair, and Tom sat down. 'I wanted to stop you from panicking. I could see you were down and thought it might help. News from home. That kind of thing. I had to do something. Didn't want you to run out on me.'

Tom looked at one of Frank's welding gloves hanging over the side of the bar. A dark stain on the thumb.

Frank pushed his glass away. 'This is all fucked, Tom. I'll be the first to admit it. If I could have saved Greg...'

'Gary, for fuck sake.'

'You're seeing this wrong, Tom. Maybe you think you can run. Survive. Escape the likes of Wayne. You don't know these people like I do. Heads like Wayne and Galloway? They come and go. They do okay, then get sloppy.' Frank shifted in his seat. 'I survived a hundred Waynes. I know how to deal with their kind. You don't. You're safe here. Safer than you imagine. A day like yesterday won't happen again. I'm ready now. Wayne won't know what hit him.'

CHAPTER FOURTEEN

STEPHANIE CAME TO Tom in his sleep. She walked through abandoned streets. Low sun casting long shadows. Skies of carnival blue. Olive trees and flowers hanging over the walls of enclosed gardens. Whitewashed walls. Her eyes were downcast. A nervous smile. She brushed her hair back with a bloodied hand. And then she was gone. He woke up in the dark. Piercing screams penetrated the blackness. His eyes filled with tears and he took the photo of Stephanie out from the bedside table. He looked at her for a while. For the first time he saw something else in her smile: anxiety; fear. The knowledge of what her future might hold.

He got up and went through to the bar. He sat close to the fire so he could no longer hear the pained cries and howls. Only the wind and the crackle of burning wood. The bucket under the leaking ceiling had filled up again. The water was brown and smelled faintly of sewage. He poured it away and replaced the bucket on its spot beneath the ceiling. He threw more logs on the fire, and watched the flames catch. He picked up the fireguard. It was very heavy. The finial in the centre resembled a peacock's plumage.

The bin behind the bar was full. He picked up the black bag and took it out to the back yard. He lifted the battered lid of one of the wheelie bins and tipped in the bottles. The leftover beer dribbled out from the bag. He went back indoors and washed his hands.

He mopped the floor behind the bar, clearing away the crumbs. The peelings and dead woodlice. He inspected the fridge and wiped up the sticky brown liquid that had dried on the shelves. A misshapen lime shorn of its peel sat in the egg holder. He left it and went back to mopping. Braudy came into the bar. His eyes were glazed and red. He was carrying snow chains and put them down on one of the tables. He wiped his nose with a frayed tissue and drew air in through his teeth.

'Those bruises look nasty,' he said.

The smell of booze drifted across the counter. Tom turned his back.

Braudy clicked shaking fingers and sat at the bar. 'Give me a whisky.'

Tom put a bottle and a glass in front of Braudy.

'Not that one.'

'Point,' said Tom.

'That one. The twelve year.'

Tom selected the bottle and set it down.

'Aren't you going to pour it?' Braudy asked, putting his elbows on the counter. 'Don't fucking skimp either.'

Tom poured out a generous measure.

Braudy raised his glass and toasted him and said, 'To the conquering hero.'

'What are you on about?'

He snapped his tongue and held the glass up to the light. 'Twelve years. Ever tried a twenty-five-year whisky?'

'No.'

'There's no difference. Chemicals stop changing after twelve years. Still fucking sell it though, don't they?' He finished the drink. He put the glass down on the counter. 'Give me another.'

Tom refilled the glass.

'Nah,' said Braudy. 'You done a number on us, Tom. You must be pretty fucking pleased with yourself. My friend in there. In that room, getting his teeth pulled out, or whatever it is they're doing to him. You've even got Frank doubting me. Questioning my fucking loyalty.'

'I didn't want any of this.'

'But you got it, Tom.' Braudy wiped his mouth with the frayed tissue.

Tom looked at the clock. It was past midday. He put the bottle of whisky back on the shelf. He squeezed out the cloth in the sink.

'Help me get the tarpaulin off Galloway's car,' said Braudy.

'I've got other things to do.'

'Don't be such a lazy fucker.'

Tom put Ken's coat on and looked for a pair of gloves but couldn't find any.

'What did you do with the gloves you borrowed?' he asked.

'Which ones?'

'The suede ones.'

'Lost them.'

'Jesus, Braudy.'

'They were your friend's gloves, weren't they?'

'Yeah.'

'No fucking loss then,' he said, picking up the snow chains.

Tom followed Braudy through the backdoor, into the snow. Smoke from the chimney rose up into the sky. A line of starlings jostled on the climbing frame. Braudy clapped his hands. The birds dispersed and Tom watched them fly away.

Braudy laid down the snow chains on an oil drum and

walked over to Galloway's car. Tom helped him clear snow off the tarpaulin.

'Know what your mistake was?' asked Braudy. 'Running. You should never have run. If you'd faced up to your responsibilities, maybe your friend would still be alive. What's his name. Greg?'

'Gary.'

'Dead, isn't he? Your bloody fault.'

'I didn't kill him.'

'On your conscience though, isn't it?'

'What do you fucking care?'

Braudy crouched down and ran his fingers under the hem of the tarpaulin. Tom knelt down and moved the bricks and the gas canister he had used to anchor down the sheet. He found the corner. Both men hauled up at the tarpaulin and allowed the snow to slide off. They heaved again and slowly drew the tarp away from the car. The tarp had scratched the silver body work. The windscreen was covered with thin layer of ice.Braudy got into the car and turned the ignition. Fleetwood Mac started to play again and he turned on the heater. He climbed out again and slammed the door. He picked up the snow chains from the oil drum.

'Need me for anything else?'

'You can fuck off now.'

Back indoors, Tom selected an old grey rug from the white cupboard, and took it through to the bar. He sat in front of the fire, and put the rug over his legs. He held out his hands, and felt the warmth return.

CHAPTER FIFTEEN

T OM WALKED AGAINST the bitter wind. The snow was knee deep in places and by the time he reached the store, his trousers and shoes were soaked through. He picked up the axe. He chopped enough wood to last a couple of days and put the axe back under the tarpaulin. He gathered the cut pieces of wood into a bin bag.

In the bar, he emptied the bag out into the basket. He took off his socks, and draped them over the radiator. After stuffing his shoes with newspaper, he placed them on the hearth. He watched the steam rise from the leather. He warmed his icy feet with his hands and squeezed at his toes until he could feel them again. The leak in the ceiling was worse; the plaster blistered and flaked. The carpet was stained from damp and gave off a heavy smell of wet fur.

He heard footsteps coming from the office. Cora walked in wearing ear plugs. She carried a red tin lockbox under her arm.

'Jesus,' she said, taking the earplugs out. 'Your toes are blue.'

He pointed at the lockbox. 'What's that?'

'Found it under a floorboard in my room,' she said, handing him the box. 'Have a look.'

He opened it and took out a makeup bag. It had a leopard print design, stained with red nail polish. A musky smell of stale perfume. The box also contained an old Polaroid camera. Sticky fluid had leaked out from the battery compartment and stung his cracked skin. She opened the makeup bag and picked out old mascara. A broken mirror. Cotton buds. A pink packet of Femidoms. Several lipsticks, all shades of cooked ham. Then she found a pouch of tobacco and some cigarette papers. In silence, she rolled a cigarette and lit it. She exhaled through her nostrils.

'Probably belonged to Frank's ex. I keep finding her things. Unopened razors. Peach soap. A bag of her drawers.'

'Leopard print?'

'Orange and lacy,' she said. 'Some guys like that colour, I suppose.'

'There's a colour for everyone.'

'Met her once. Mandy. Sour. Hard-looking ticket. Painted-on eyebrows. Took a lot of Valium.'

'Tucker liked her, didn't he?'

'Make of that what you will.' She got a drink of water and sat back down near the fire. She flicked her cigarette on to the burning logs. 'I don't think Frank meant to break up with her. He'd take her back if he could.'

They heard whistling. The door opened and Frank came in, wiping his nose with a handkerchief. He was wearing a beige PVC apron. He took off his leather welding gloves and scowled at Tom. Frank tore off a length of blue kitchen paper, dried his hands, and came over to the bar. He trailed his hand across Cora's back and poured himself a thick measure of brandy. He pointed at the socks on the radiator. 'Whose are they?'

'Mine,' said Tom.

He threw the socks at Tom. 'Either of you seen Braudy?'

'Not for a while.'

He saw the lockbox and picked it up. 'This yours?'

144

'Found it in my room,' said Cora.

'Was there anything else in this?'

'Just the camera and the makeup bag.'

'You better not be lying to me.'

'I'm not.'

Frank examined the camera. He touched the point where the battery had leaked and rubbed the discharge between finger and thumb. He wiped his hand on his apron and put the camera back in the box. Cora gave him make-up bag. He looked through it and pulled out the Femidoms.

'What the fuck are these?'

'Come on, Frank. You're a big boy now,' said Cora.

Tom looked down to hide his smile.

'Something funny, Tom?' asked Frank.

'Nothing's funny.'

He clicked his fingers. 'Get that box. Come with me.'

Tom put on his wet socks. His shoes had stiffened from drying. He picked up the box. Frank pushed him through to the office. Tom could see the broken trophies sitting on one of the workbenches. The plastic figures were laid out neatly on a green paper towel. Frank grabbed him by the collar. Tom could smell his stale breath.

'Don't appreciate you joking around like that,' he said. 'Laughing at me.'

'Didn't mean anything by it.'

'You're not as clever as you think, Tom.'

Frank's eyes steadied and straightened the collar of Tom's T-shirt. He walked down the corridor and Tom followed him. They reached the safe room. A hammering sound came from within. There was a crinkle of plastic. A sticky scratch of duct tape being pulled from a roll.

Frank entered the room and beckoned Tom forward with a thick finger. The blue shower curtain was splashed with blood. The plastic sheeting on the floor was covered in shit and purple vomit. Near the back wall, Galloway and Tucker lay face down. Both men were naked. Their hands were tied behind their backs and they had white paint on their shoulders and jaws. They both had the drooping mouths of elderly men. Tucker had been blinded in his one good eye. The skin on his chest was scalded and blistered.

Frank whistled. The two men stood up. Frank whistled again and they turned to face him. He clapped his hands. The two men sat down on the floor. Tom turned away.

Frank said to Tom, 'Look a bit pale, there? Smell getting to you?'

He nodded.

'Ken here chews gum with his mouth open.'

'Works a charm,' said Ken, throwing some bloodied paper towels into a plastic shopping bag.

Tom spat on the floor. He held his hand over his mouth and retched. His eyes watered.

'See anything funny here?' asked Frank.

'No.'

Frank smirked and said to Ken, 'Start cleaning this up, mate. Hose it down a bit.'

'Bit of bleach?'

'Later.'

Ken left the room. Frank dropped the box into the shopping bag. He handed it to Tom. It was heavy and smelled of meat.

'Take it out to the incinerator.'

'What about the batteries?' asked Tom.

'What batteries?'

'The ones in the camera. You're not supposed to burn them.'

'Just fucking do it,' said Frank. 'And once you're done go and get some shovels.'

'How many?'

'Three. No. Two.'

Tom left the room. He told himself to keep breathing slowly and deeply. He was careful not to look in the plastic bag. Back in the office, Braudy was sitting with his back to the wall of old calendars. He held a hand over his infected ear. Eyes red and wet from tears. Tom carried on through to the bar. He took in the scent of burning wood and beer-soaked carpets. Water dripped slowly into the iron bucket by the pool table. He tried not to think of Galloway and Tucker. Their silence. Their injuries.

He went through the backdoor to the coal shed. Some of the snow had melted around the doorway. He put the bag in the incinerator. The heat nauseated him and he returned outside and took in the chilly air. After a few minutes, he heard people talking. He fetched the shovels from the store. Ken emerged from the Bothy carrying a bottle of engine oil and a toolbox. He opened up the truck and popped open the truck bonnet. Tom took the shovels over to him.

'Where's the other shovel?' he asked as he checked the oil.

'Frank only wanted two.'

'Put them on the flatbed.'

Tom dropped the shovels in the back and waited. Ken finished, unhooked the prop, and closed the bonnet. From his toolbox, he brought out a small jar of Swarfega. He unscrewed the lid and smeared a dollop of green jelly on to his filthy hands.

'You got gloves?' he asked.

'Yeah.'

'Put them on. And your hat.'

'I don't have a hat.'

'One in the glove compartment. Make sure you wear it.'

Ken knelt down and rubbed his hands in the snow. The green-black jelly came off. He dried his hands with a dirty rag.

Something caught Tom's eye. He saw Cora standing at her bedroom window. She held a red hot water bottle to her chest. Tom raised his hand, and she waved back. Ken shook his head. 'Leave it out, Tom.'

They heard a shout. Frank stepped out from the Bothy. He wore a sheepskin coat and held a sawn-off shotgun in his arms. Galloway and Tucker emerged from the back door, stumbling over the snow. Both men were naked and bloodied. Tucker had his hand on Galloway's shoulder so he could tell which way to go.

Braudy followed the two men out. He was wearing a big red Puffa jacket that made his head look small. In his right hand he held a pistol loosely, almost like it was too heavy to lift.

Frank whistled at the two men and they raised their heads like well trained dogs. He pushed them towards Galloway's car and they shambled towards it. Frank opened the boot.

'Right.' He pointed at Galloway. 'You. In.'

Galloway moved forward, and Frank pushed him into the boot. Tucker crawled in after him. Frank slammed the boot shut and picked up his sawn-off.

'Okay, Braudy. Get in the car. Put blowers on.'

Braudy clumsily holstered the pistol in his belt and climbed into the passenger seat. Frank got into the car. He opened the window.

'You got keys, Frank?' asked Ken.

'Yeah. You?'

Ken held up his set.

'Don't bloody lose them. And take it canny. Okay?'

Tom and Ken got into the truck. The leather seats were cold. Ken started up the engine, turned on the heaters, and opened the glove compartment. He pulled out a Leeds United bobble hat and handed it to Tom.

'You look like a Wednesday man. Are you?'

'Wednesday? No.' Tom put the hat on. The fabric itched.

'That's something at least.' He reversed the truck out into the road. They started off slowly, waiting for Frank to catch them up. Ken picked at his ear. The sock monkey charm hanging from the rearview mirror swayed back and forth.

'You need to wise up,' said Ken.

'In what way?'

'Stop taking the piss,' he said. 'And stop acting ungrateful.'

'I've done nothing wrong.'

'Keep saying that, don't you? Yet here you are,' said Ken. 'Thing is you *hope* you've done nothing wrong. Take a few minutes ago. You and Cora. She was looking out of the window at you. She waved. You waved back. If it was me and you were waving at my girlfriend...'

'Jesus, Ken.'

'You talk with her. All the fucking time.'

'I talk to you all the fucking time too.'

'Other day, Braudy saw you walking back together. Over the hill.'

'Frank sent me because he was busy.'

Ken tried the brakes. The truck fishtailed a little. 'All I'm trying to say is you might want to start taking a look around you. Think about your actions, how they might look. No secret that Tucker had his suspicions about you. We all have.'

'What about Frank?'

'No. Not him. And that's the strange thing. You're the first fucker to come up here and not be treated like shit by him.'

The road wound through the moorland and lead down to the Ladybower reservoir. In the afternoon light, the water looked like smoked glass. Trees lined the hills. Dark branches arched over white roads, ready to scoop up the unwary rambler, the careless cyclist. The road ran close to the water. They drove up a narrow lane which cut through a small forest.

Ken parked the truck and they got out. Tom got the shovels and watched Frank drive Galloway's car up the lane. Tom could hear the muffled sound of a car radio with the volume turned up high. Frank killed the engine and got out of the car. He had a handkerchief clamped over his nose. Braudy stumbled out of the passenger door, fell to his knees and vomited on to the snow.

'State of him,' said Ken.

Frank opened the boot and whistled. The two men climbed out, unsteady on their feet, no longer aware of the cold. Galloway looked around blinking. Tucker wiped blood from his blinded eye. His skin the colour of butter against the white of the snow. He reached out and put his hand on Galloway's shoulder. They both walked forward slowly across the uneven ground.

Frank handed over the sawn-off shotgun to Ken and said, 'Keep them honest.'

'Will do.'

He blew his nose and pointed at Tom and Braudy. 'Come on. Let's go.'

Tom picked up the two shovels and walked up the grass

verge into the wood. Frank displaced snow as he brushed past branches. Snow and ice fell from the trees. He could hear Braudy's breathing and Ken's footsteps. Galloway and Tucker were ten or twenty paces behind him.

Frank looked over his shoulder. 'Nice woods, these.'

Tom heard something jumping from branch to branch. A twig snapped. More snow was dislodged from above.

'Few nice clearings. Good place for a picnic. A summer's day. You one for eating outside, Tom?'

'Not so much.'

There was a loud crack to the right. Something thawing, something loosening. The woods no longer still. There was another noise behind Tom. He turned back. Braudy's eyes were downturned. His lips moved. No words came out.

'Ah. Here.' Frank pointed towards a point where the trees thinned out. 'This will do.'

They stepped past the pines and into a small clearing four or five metres wide. Pine needles poked up through the points where the snow was thinner.

'Put the shovels down.' He nodded towards a fallen log. 'Take a seat.'

Tom sat down and watched Braudy come through the trees. Frank patted Braudy on the shoulder. Ken pushed Galloway and Tucker into the centre of the clearing. The two men stood there. Bloodied, bruised. Shivering.

Frank marked out a rectangle in the snow, two metres by two. He whistled at Galloway and Tucker and they walked over towards him. He handed them the shovels. No-one had to ask them to dig.

Frank lit a cigarette while Ken prowled around the edge of the clearing. He held the sawn-off close to his chest. Braudy looked on, leaning on a tree, holding his infected ear. Tom looked upwards and saw only small patches of blue above the tangled branches.

It took Galloway and Tucker half an hour to dig about a metre downwards. After another ten minutes, Frank told them to stop. Ken took the shovels away and leaned them up against a tree. Frank unbuttoned his coat and took out a pistol. He strolled over to Galloway and shot him in the head. Dark blood spattered the ground. The body fell into the hole. Tom tried to focus on the bird tracks in the snow. The frost on the branches. Hoping that his mind would not record the horror or the pain. He heard Tucker begin to cry.

Frank handed Braudy the pistol. 'Let's draw a line under this.'

Braudy looked at Galloway's corpse.

'Finish off Tucker. Show me you're not in on this with him.'

'I'm not.'

'Then show me.'

'I don't know if I can, Frank.'

'It's just like we said on the way over here, remember?'

Braudy looked at the pistol and held it tight in his band-aged hand.

'Get this done and we'll have a nice dinner,' he said. 'A few drinks. Put it all behind us.'

Braudy nodded again but did not move. He looked over at Tom. His bottom lip trembled.

Frank reached out and lifted Braudy's shaking hand so he pointed the pistol at Tucker's head.

'It's a matter of loyalty. Words are no good.' Frank stepped back.

'I can't.'

'Can't or won't?'

Braudy let the gun fall down to his side.

Frank rubbed at his eye and pinched the bridge of his nose. 'Mate. Lift the gun again.'

'No.'

Frank snapped his fingers at Ken who handed him the sawn-off. He released the safety catch and pointed the gun at Braudy. 'Can't or won't?'

'Frank—'

'Don't make me bury you too.'

Braudy wiped his eyes and cocked the hammer. He pushed the pistol against the back of Tucker's head and shut his eyes. He squeezed the trigger. There was a damp fizz. No bang.

Braudy opened his eyes. His arm relaxed and the pistol moved. There was a bang. The bullet took off Tucker's left ear. He stumbled and fell forward into the hole. He howled. Blood spurted from the wound.

Frank stepped forward and blasted Tucker with the sawn-off. Snow fell quietly from the trees. He took the pistol off Braudy and reached out to make sure he didn't fall. Furious, he looked back at Ken and shouted, 'Did you test the fucking ammunition?'

'Yes, I fucking tested it.'

Frank held up the pistol and fired it again. There was another hangfire.

'Maybe it got some water in it,' said Ken.

'Jesus. Fucking details, Ken.'

'I checked. I promise.'

Frank led Braudy away from the open grave, whispering assurances. Ken handed a shovel to Tom.

'Ken,' said Frank. 'Come and get us when you're done here. We'll be by the lake.'

'I'm sorry about the gun.'

'No more mistakes. Okay?'

Frank caught up with Braudy and they went back towards the cars.

'Come on, Tom. We're up,' said Ken. They stood over the grave and shovelled dirt and bloodied snow over the bodies. Tom tried not to look at the men's injuries.

After ten minutes, Ken rested on his shovel and wiped sweat from his forehead. Tom carried on shovelling.

'Nothing wrong with that ammunition,' said Ken. 'Tested it myself.'

'Are you sure there isn't a better way?'

'Fuck off, Tom. Nothing wrong with the test. I won't hear the end of this now.'

Tom kept filling the hole with soil and snow. His arms started to ache. He stopped for a rest.

'I'll finish here, Tom. You go back to the truck.'

'Keys?'

'Keys stay with me, mate. Doors are open.'

Tom picked up his shovel and made his way back towards the truck. He followed the footsteps and the points where snow had fallen from the branches. Here and there, he could see spots of dark red against the white. He reached the lane, and climbed down the shallow embankment. Galloway's car had gone.

Tom threw his shovel on to the flatbed and washed his hands and face with snow. He got into the truck and put his gloves back on. There was a strange chemical smell. He could almost taste it. The road was in shadow. He closed his eyes and saw the spray of blood. The stained snow. The dull crack of gunshot. He opened his eyes and saw Ken emerge from the woods. He was whistling. A few startled crows flew upwards into the darkening sky.

Ken threw his shovel on to the flatbed of the truck, climbed in, and started up the engine. He turned the truck around slowly and they drove back to the main road and returned to the reservoir. Tom saw a finger of black smoke rising up into the chilly air. After a mile they saw Frank and Braudy standing by the side of the road. Both men had changed into boiler suits and placed their soiled clothes in a rubble sack. Galloway's car was burning. The bodywork was black and the tyres had started to melt into the tarmac. Tom could smell the rubber.

Braudy's eyes were red from tears. His nose was running.

'Okay, Tom,' said Frank. 'Shift yourself into the back.'

Tom took off his seat belt and clambered into the cramped space behind the front seats. Braudy sat next to him and looked straight ahead. Frank got in the passenger seat and blew into his hands. He scratched at the white wiry hairs on the back of his neck.

'I could do with a whisky,' said Ken.

'Let's see about these blowers. See if we can't all warm up a bit.'

Ken started up the truck again and performed a U-turn in the road. They headed back towards the Bothy. The hills were dark. The sky was grey and heavy. There would be more snow.

'Tell you what, Ken. Galloway's car was a beauty.'

'Good power on it, I expect,' said Ken.

Frank turned around. 'Getting the heat in the back?'

'Yeah,' said Tom.

Braudy touched the cotton wool in his ear.

'Engine was quiet. Like a whisper,' said Frank. 'And that dashboard. It was something else.'

'GPS?' asked Ken.

'Oh, aye. And then some.'

'And a smooth drive?'

'The smoothest.' Frank laughed. 'You fellas okay back there?'

Tom nodded. Braudy said nothing.

CHAPTER SIXTEEN

TOM THREW FRANK and Braudy's soiled clothes into the incinerator. He watched the flames. The heat forced tears from his eyes. He wondered how long he could stay out here. Away from the others. It was still snowing heavily and the wind made him shiver. Night would soon fall. Across the yard, the store lights were on. Frank was inside, moving things about.

Tom went over and knocked on the filthy windows.

'Where the fuck have you been, Braudy?' shouted Frank. He came to the door. His eyes were watery and sunken. Tom could smell alcohol on his breath.

'You seen Braudy?' asked Frank.

'Think he's keeping his head down.'

'So?'

'He might need some space. After today.'

'Fuck off, Tom. Save the bleeding heart shit and give me a hand in here.'

Tom moved two red watering cans over to a stack of clay plant pots. He moved offcuts of roof insulation away from the door and then helped Frank shift a few sacks of grit from the back of the store. When it was done, Tom went back indoors. He took his coat and shoes off and sat down near the fire. The blackened limbs of burning branches shifted on the grate.

Ken sipped at a glass of whisky. He had taken off his shoes and socks. His feet were swollen. Two boxes of ammunition sat on one of the long tables.

'You look like shit,' said Ken. 'Have a drink.'

'In a bit.'

'It'll do you some good,' he said, touching his feet. He winced and sucked back his whisky. 'Couldn't do me a favour, could you?'

'What?'

'Get me some socks from the fridge. Feet are killing me.'

In the office, Tom stood by a workbench for a second to compose himself. His hands shook. He thought of the misfiring gun and the spray of blood as Tucker fell on top of Galloway's corpse. He looked at the calendars on the wall. The photos of the women offering a lurid vision of paradise. Vacant smiles, perfect teeth. He wondered what they were doing now. He heard singing coming from the kitchen. He carried on down the corridor and passed the laundry room. The washing machine was on and there was a smell of bleach. A washing line had been strung up between hooks on the wall. Underwear hung from brightly coloured pegs. Thick towels dried on a spindly clothes horse.

In the kitchen, Cora was reading at the table and singing softly to herself. She put down her book and smiled. He fought back tears and she handed him a tissue. It smelled of lavender. She switched on the kettle while he dried his eyes. He sat down and Cora brought him an instant coffee. A few granules floated on the surface.

'Wayne will come up here soon. Won't he?' asked Tom.

She nodded and touched his hand. He drank his coffee. It was hot and sweet.

'You know Frank won't be able to protect you for much longer.'

'There's nowhere to run to.'

'That's the first step, isn't it? Realising you have to move on.'

'Is it?'

'We can find somewhere,' she said, touching his hand again.

He opened one of the fridges and picked out a pair of stripy blue socks and placed the stool back in the corner. He left the kitchen and went to the toilet opposite his bedroom. After washing his face and his hands, he looked in the mirror. The bruises around his eyes were yellow-black. He looked old.

He returned to the bar. Ken was soaking his feet in a plastic bowl. 'What took you so long?' he asked.

'Cora was in the kitchen,' he said, handing over the socks.

'What was she doing?'

'Reading.'

'Magazine?'

'Book.'

Ken took his feet out of the plastic bowl and wiped his feet on the carpet. He put on the socks and wiggled his toes. He sighed with relief and laid out a sheet of newspaper on a table. He carried in the trophies, the broken plastic figures, and a small tube of glue. Carefully, he mended each trophy, making sure that each plastic figure was glued in place. He noticed that one of the figures was missing a head. He swore.

'I think it was like that before,' said Tom.

'It wasn't,' replied Ken.

The lights flickered and faded. Ken groaned and the power cut out. He got up, opened a drawer behind the bar, and took out a box of candles. He lit them and placed them on tables and shelves.

In the half-light Braudy came into the room dressed in jogging bottoms and a red wool jumper. He poured himself a pint of vodka and studied Ken for a few moments before sitting near the front door. He gazed at the pale candlelight reflected in the windows. He was saying something under his breath. Tom could not hear what.

Ken opened the metal boxes of ammunition. He sat at the counter and took out a handful of shotgun cartridges. He rolled the red waxy surface of a cartridge between thumb and forefinger, and then shook it close to his ear. He put the cartridge in an old grey shoe box.

Cora came into the bar holding a torch. She walked around the pool table and tripped accidentally on the iron bucket. Water sloshed on to the carpet.

'Empty that, Tom,' said Ken, as he checked another cartridge.

Tom picked up the bucket and took it outside. The snow had started to cover the tyre tracks and footprints. He stood there and let the cold air clear his head. He looked through the windows at Cora. She was moving some of the candles around. He thought about what she had said and wondered if it was a trick. Some test of loyalty devised by Frank.

Tom emptied the water into a drain and stepped back into the bar. He brushed snow from his hair and put the bucket back in its place.

'Any sign of Frank?' asked Ken.

'Still in the store.'

'Get yourself a beer,' said Ken. 'Frank will expect you to drink.'

Tom took a beer from the fridge. The bottle wasn't very cold.

'Get Cora one too.'

Tom picked out another bottle and handed it to her. She was standing by the pool table, rolling the cue ball up and down the baize.

'You any good at pool?' asked Cora.

'Wouldn't say I'm good.'

She handed him a cue. 'Come on. Loser has to wash Ken's feet.'

Tom racked the balls. Cora selected a cue and took the break. She split the pack well. Tom picked up the cube of chalk and held it in his hand while he chose his shot. Frank came in from outside, snow melting on his shoulders. He took off his gloves and coat. He was wearing an old black tracksuit. It was shiny at the knees and elbows. He picked up a bottle of whisky from behind the bar and poured himself a tall glass. He looked at the trophies Ken had fixed.

'Where's the head on this one?'

'I'll find it when the lights come back on.'

Frank looked at Braudy and said, 'Where were you? Thought you were going to help us move some stuff in the store.'

'I needed a shower,' replied Braudy, hunching his shoulders.

'So it was okay for me to do your fucking work?'

'Come on, Frank,' said Tom. 'Give him a break.'

'You can fuck off as well,' replied Frank. He sneezed and wiped his nose on the back of his sleeve.

Braudy finished his drink. With shaking hands, he helped himself to the last of the vodka. Some splashed on to the table.

Frank looked at Tom strangely, and said, 'Don't know how you two are playing in this light.'

'It's not too bad.'

'She winning?'

'Early days,' said Tom. He took his shot and missed.

'You still have that game, Ken?'

'Which game?'

'Board game. With the dice.'

'Threw it out. Board got wet. A leak somewhere. Ruined it.'

'You could get that deck of cards. We could have a game of poker. Or – fuck it – what's it called? Cribbage.'

'Forgotten the rules,' said Ken.

Cora wandered around the table humming to herself and checking angles. Frank emptied his glass of whisky and scowled. 'What are you so cheerful about?'

'Good to play against a worthy competitor,' she said, taking another shot. The ball cannoned in off the four ball with a satisfying click.

'There's an easy shot. Top left,' said Frank.

She potted the three ball in the opposite corner and walked the long way round the table. Tom rested the thick end of his cue on his foot.

Frank opened the fridge and took out a bottle. 'This is warm. Here, Tom. Was your beer warm?'

'It was okay.'

'Can't drink this. It'll taste like filth.'

'Let me put the beers outside for a while,' said Ken. 'Snow will do the trick.'

Frank returned to his barstool. Ken picked up a few bottles and took them outside. Braudy stared at Tom and mumbled to himself. A wry smile formed on his lips.

Ken came back in, stamping snow from his shoes.

Frank filled his glass with more whisky. 'Easy one for you there, Tom. Glance off the five ball.'

'Trying to avoid the tear if I can,' said Tom.

'Are you letting her win?'

'No.'

Frank turned to Ken, and said, 'You should teach Tom how to test ammunition.'

'I don't know anything about guns,' said Tom.

'You don't need to know about guns to test bullets,' said Frank.

Cora bent down to take another shot. Frank stared at her behind and sipped his whisky. She struck the cue ball hard. The ball hit the jaws of the pocket and rolled away to the centre of the table.

'Unlucky,' said Tom. He chalked the tip of his cue and bent down to take the shot. He aimed at the bottom of the cue ball and struck it hard. It hit its target and then screwed back dramatically into the middle pocket.

Cora laughed and patted him on the shoulder. 'You have much to learn.'

'Go out and see if those beers are cold yet, Tom,' said Frank.

Tom put his cue back in the rack and crossed the room. He opened the front door and saw five bottles of beer sitting in a small mound of snow. He picked up a bottle and took it back inside.

Frank opened it, took a sip, and said, 'Not that cold, is it?'

'Coldest one there.'

Frank went around the counter and brought out a jar of pickled eggs and opened the lid. He picked up a few packets of cheese and onion crisps and put them out on the bar.

Tom returned to the pool table and Cora took her shot. The ball rolled over the tear in the baize, and was deflected away and came to rest next to the cushion.

'Shite.'

Frank reached in and plucked out an egg from the jar. He ate half of it and chewed away, still watching Cora. 'This isn't a very lady-like game, Cora.'

'You what?'

'Lady-like.'

'What's lady-like? In your fucking book?'

Frank thought for a moment. 'Darts. At least you don't have to bend over showing your arse to everyone with darts.'

'Stop being a dick, Frank,' she said.

Frank turned away, disgusted. He ate the other half of the egg. His jaw cracked as he chewed. 'How many beers are you on now, Tom?' he asked.

'Second.'

'Turning into a fucking woman now?'

'Pacing myself.'

Braudy shivered. He looked at the bottle of vodka and stood up. His knees buckled. He took a moment to steady himself. Then he lifted up his glass and cleared his throat. He said, 'None of you have said anything. About Tucker. About what happened today.'

'Sit down, Braudy,' said Frank.

'I want to talk about him.'

'Well, we bloody don't,' said Ken. 'He's old news. Forget him.'

Braudy put his glass down heavily on the table. 'You can't even bring yourself to say his name. Can you?'

'You're drunk.'

'And you're ashamed of what you did. Aren't you? Torturing your own fucking friend.'

'He wasn't a friend,' replied Ken.

'He was to me.' Braudy wiped his mouth on the sleeve of his red jumper and smiled sadly. 'My friend – my friend is dead. And Tom over there is alive. Lying. Taking you all for a fucking ride.'

There was a click. The power came back on. Tom blinked in the bright light.

Braudy sat down and lifted his glass. Quietly, he said, 'To Tucker.'

Cora blew out the candle in front of her. Tom smelled hot wax and watched a pale thread of smoke rise from the wick. Frank opened a bag of crisps and ate them slowly.

Tom picked up his cue. He took a shot. Missed. Cora quickly cleared the table. She screwed back neatly to leave her on for the eight ball. She potted it and held her hand out to Tom.

'You're in luck, Ken,' she said. 'His hands are like sandpaper. Sort those corns out nicely.'

'Fuck off,' replied Ken.

She put her beer bottle on the bar and lit a cigarette.

Frank clicked his fingers and pointed at Braudy. 'Get the girl another beer from outside. And one for Tom.'

'I think I might be all right with this one,' said Tom.

'Fuck off. You're having another drink. The both of you,' he said. 'Make yourself useful, Braudy. Get some beers from outside.'

Braudy finished his drink and staggered through the front door. Ken looked up from one of the boxes of ammunition. He took a sip from his glass but realised there was no whisky in it. He reached for the bottle and looked at the label.

'Twelve years,' he said.

'You should try it with some water,' said Frank.

'It'll go cloudy.'

Frank turned around in his stool and looked towards the door. 'Where's Braudy with that fucking beer?'

Cora laughed and said, 'Fuck sake. You're on one tonight.'

Frank raised his finger and pointed at her. 'Another fucking word, Cora, and I swear I'll bury you.'

'Frank,' said Tom.

'Button it.' Frank glared at Cora. 'Another word. From either of you. Understand?'

Tom picked up a log from the basket and placed it on the fire. Cora took the brass poker and moved the wood so that it rested on the embers.

Ken got out of his seat and stared out of the window. 'Can't see him out there.'

Frank groaned and rubbed at his eyes. 'Go and have a look, Tom.'

Tom went outside. The snow stung Tom's face. He saw there were still four bottles sticking out of the snow. He peered into the darkness.

'Braudy!'

Footsteps in the snow led away from the Bothy. Tom called out again. There was no reply. He went back indoors. Frank and Ken looked up from their drinks.

'He's gone,' said Tom.

'In that? Fuck off,' said Frank.

'He'll come back,' replied Ken. 'Too bloody cold for the soft bastard.'

Cora moved away from the fire and looked at her watch. 'He's been how long? Five minutes? He might be lost.'

Frank snapped his fingers. 'Go and find him, Tom.'

'Me?'

'You were the one bleating on about how you felt fucking sorry for him.'

'I'll come with you, Tom,' said Cora.

'You sit there. Don't move a fucking muscle. Tom's going. That's the end of it.'

Tom found a torch and some mittens. He went to the lobby and put on boots and a thick coat. He took another coat to give to Braudy and stepped outside into the snow and freezing winds. Braudy's trail of footprints led across the yard, and out to the road. Tom saw splashes of orange vomit in the snow. He called out again over the wind. The light from his torch flickered and he tapped it until the beam was steady. The snow came up to his ankles. Further up the road it reached his knees. Tom crossed over to the other side and saw a half-concealed object. It was a red jumper. He called out again. The wind swirled around him and he was briefly blinded by the snow. He stopped and looked towards the Bothy. The lights went out. The strange, uneven angles of its structure replaced by darkness. He looked at the trail of footprints, afraid that they too might vanish. They veered left towards a stone wall where knee-high drifts had formed. He pointed the torch towards the field and saw a shape shambling away from him.

'Braudy!'

Tom climbed over the wall. The footsteps in the snow were closer together. He looked back to where he thought the Bothy was. There was a faint glow. He trudged onwards and followed the trail up a hill. A pair of boots had been thrown to one side. Tom picked up the boots. He tied the laces together and slung the boots over his shoulders. His face had gone numb.

Squinting into the wind, he spotted the figure floundering through deep snow. Tom did not bother shouting out. He walked as fast as he could, breathing hard and muttering under his breath. He lifted his torch and saw Braudy had fallen face down. He was no longer moving.

The drifts of snow were deep. He held out his arms for balance. The wind whipped around him. His lungs burned and his legs ached. In the middle of the field, the snow reached Tom's thighs. When he reached Braudy, he rolled him on to his back. His purple Bread T-shirt was soaked through. His feet were bare. He helped Braudy into the spare coat and the boots. He lifted him up and helped him walk.

'Keep going, you stupid bastard,' said Tom. 'Don't make me carry you.'

The wind was at their backs. Braudy limped along. His lips drawn back. Teeth chattering. He started to moan. The words unclear but muttered with drunken savagery. Tom told him to shut up. He told him to walk properly. He told him to stop being a useless sack of shit. He told him to stop feeling sorry for himself.

When they reached the bottom of the hill the Bothy's lights came back on. The orange sodium lamps shone through the falling snow, producing an eerie, sickly glow. Tom put Braudy against a stone wall to shelter him from the wind. He tried to catch his breath. His thighs ached and he could no longer feel his fingers or toes.

He picked Braudy up again and they carried on along the

road. After fifty metres Braudy tripped and fell over. Tom hauled him back to his feet and shouted at him in frustration. He told him how glad he was that Tucker was dead. His voice grew hoarse and he told him how he wished he had stayed at home. How he missed Stephanie. How he felt responsible for her death. How he wished he had done more. The storm drowned out the words. Even Tom was unsure about what he had said.

When they reached the Bothy, Ken and Cora came out to help. They carried Braudy through to the bar and put him in front of the fire. He was nearly unconscious. His skin was red and had already started to blister.

'Did the stupid bastard get lost?' asked Ken.

'I don't think so,' said Tom.

'He needs to warm up,' said Cora.

'He's near the fire. He'll be okay. Daft twat,' said Frank.

Cora glared at him and helped Ken take off Braudy's shoes and wet clothes.

Tom walked over to one of the radiators and pulled off his gloves. His fingers were numb. He took off his coat and boots. His wet, foul-smelling socks. He felt very hungry and tired. Frank came over to him and handed him a glass of brandy. He sipped at it. The alcohol burned his lips.

'Is he conscious?' asked Tom.

'Just about,' replied Cora.

'Go and put him in bed. He'll warm up,' said Frank.

'It might be an idea to give him a hot shower,' replied Ken.

'Then do that. Just get the cunt out of my sight.'

Ken and Cora lifted Braudy to his feet, and helped him out of the room. Frank walked past Tom and eased himself down on to a barstool. He stared at the trophies Ken had fixed.

'He nearly died, Frank,' said Tom.

'You can stop being a cunt and all. Drink your brandy and fuck off.'

Tom could hear the wind outside. It was getting stronger.

Tom returned to his bedroom. There was a cup of cold coffee on his bedside table. He ran the bath and undressed. He stood there, watching the steam rise up from the water. He climbed into the tub. The hot water made his skin sting. He waited for his body to acclimatise to the heat. He picked up the disc of soap and scrubbed at his body and face. Then he lay back and looked up at the stained ceiling and felt sweat on his brow.

There was a knock at the door. It was Cora. She was holding two pink towels.

'Thought you'd like these,' she said. 'They're fresh.'

'You didn't need to do that.'

'Where do you want them?'

'Throw them on the chair.'

She hesitated for a moment and then came into the room. She put the towels down and saw the cup of cold coffee on the bedside table.

'Do you want a drink or anything?' she asked. 'Just to warm you up.'

'I'll be okay,' he said.

'I can reheat that coffee.'

'Is Braudy okay?'

'Not sure.'

'You should go back. In case Frank says something.'

She paused for a moment and then left the room. He heard her walk back up the corridor.

He pulled out the bath plug and dried himself with the soft, sweet smelling towels. After changing into his pyjamas he got under the duvet. He fell asleep quickly and did not dream.

CHAPTER SEVENTEEN

TOM AWOKE IN the dark and could hear snoring. He switched on his bedside light. Frank was asleep on the silk chair at the end of the bed. His head was lolling forward. A string of drool hung from his lips. He had stretched out and wore no shoes or socks. His toes were hairy. The nails were long and jagged. He yawned, shifted in the chair, and then lifted his head. It took a moment for him to remember where he was. He nodded at Tom and then wiped his nose and mouth with a grey handkerchief.

'Is everything okay, Frank?'

'Give me a minute.'

Tom moved his pillows up against the wall. His legs ached and he winced as he propped himself up. The broken bedspring jabbed into his side.

Frank took out a cigarette and tried to light it with his Dupont. The flint sparked but there was no flame.

'Fucking thing,' he said, shaking it.

Tom opened the drawer in his bedside table. He found the book of matches and handed it to Frank. He tore out a match, struck it, and lit his cigarette. He looked at the design on the front of the matchbook. He smiled.

'Had these done for a place called Piraya. A massage parlour. I owned it with Wayne. Ten years ago or so. Thai girls with wrists like tree trunks. Used to have police constables coming in for freebies. All sorts.' He looked around the room and sniffed. 'It smells like drains in here.'

Tom moved himself so the broken bedspring wasn't poking into his leg. Frank smoked his cigarette down to the filter. He looked at the newspapers pasted on the wall. He stubbed out the cigarette and flicked the butt towards the bath tub. It missed and landed in the middle of the room. He pocketed the book of matches and reclined in the chair. His eyes closed for a moment and then he murmured, 'Ken says Braudy's got frostbite. Daft bastard was crying when he was put to bed.'

Tom saw movement beneath the bath and heard something moving around in the walls. It made his skin itch.

'I'm sorry I sent you out there,' said Frank.

'I don't think he even wanted to be rescued,' replied Tom.

Frank crossed his legs and sat back in the chair.

'Not bad for your back, this. Tried sitting in it?'

'No.'

'It's comfy,' he said, patting the torn silk. 'Comfy but firm.'

Tom pulled the duvet up to his chest. He pushed himself up so his legs didn't ache as much.

'Mandy found it. Five years ago. Over in an antiques shop in Macclesfield. She wanted a chest of drawers. Something art deco. Ended up with this instead.' Frank stood up and snapped his fingers. 'Come on. Pack your stuff.'

'What?'

'Go up to Tucker's room. It's no good down here.'

'Now?'

'Get your stuff packed.'

Tom got up and put on his jeans. Frank lit another cigarette and got himself up off the chair. He took a moment to steady himself. Tom packed up his clothes and wrapped up the duvet, the pillows, the towels. Then he shouldered his rucksack, and followed Frank up the corridor.

In the office, Ken was sitting on a workbench and swigging a bottle of whisky. He had laid out two dismantled Smith and Wessons on an oily cloth. He put the cap back on the bottle. His red eyes were half-closed.

Frank belched and then held his hand over his mouth for a few seconds. He sat down on a desk and said, 'Take Tom up to Tucker's room. No good where he's sleeping now. Smells of fucking drains.'

'It smells worse in Tucker's.'

Frank opened a drawer and handed Tom a roll of bin bags. 'Throw out any stuff you don't want. Clothes. Anything. Give him a hand with his stuff, Ken.'

Ken swigged some whisky and leaned back against the workbench. He scraped at the label with his finger.

'I should get you a fresh towel,' said Ken.

'I have some.' He held up the pink towels.

'Who gave you those?'

'Cora.'

Tom followed Ken up the stairs. He saw the small magazine rack had been filled with old issues of *Exchange and Mart*. Ken walked over to the white door covered in old football stickers. He opened the door and switched on the light. The room had a single bed and a small lamp on a bedside table. A pine chair with splayed legs sat near the window. Opposite it, a handsome oak wardrobe was pushed into the corner. The wallpaper had a pattern of old fighter planes, all swooping downwards, guns firing.

'I'll see if we have any air freshener,' said Ken.

'Can I open the windows?' asked Tom.

'Nah. Frames have buckled.' He dropped the duvet and pillow on the bed, and went over to the oak wardrobe. It was full of tracksuits, old jumpers, and pastel shaded shirts. 'You can have these if you like,' he said.

'I'll see,' said Tom.

Ken closed the wardrobe door and left the room. Tom pressed down on the mattress. It was soft and dipped in the middle. The carpet was threadbare and rotten sections had been cut away to reveal floorboards. He looked at the wall and saw a small framed picture of a naked girl. On the bottom of the frame a name had been printed on black embossing tape: 'CHLOE'. She had blonde matted hair, offering a smile, uncertain what the immediate future would hold for her. Tom tore off a bin liner from the roll. He binned the picture and cleared the mess from beneath the bed. Crisp packets, some odd socks. A roll of cling film. An empty milk bottle.

He stripped the bed and laid out the sheet on the stained mattress and tucked in the sides. He put the duvet down over the sheets. In the bedside cabinet he found a pouch of rolling tobacco, some papers, and a box of candles. In the drawer, there was an open packet of flavoured condoms, a torn copy of *Treasure Island*, and a torch.

He took the photo of Stephanie out of his wallet. Some parts of the image had rubbed off. He hid the picture in the book and threw the condoms away. Then, he opened the wardrobe and thumbed through the tracksuits. He could smell moth balls and ammonia. On the top shelf there was a collection of wool hats. All black with white stitching. He pushed the tracksuits aside and saw a couple of whalebone corsets hooked over a hanger. He left the clothes alone and looked at the bottom shelf. He found several pairs of workmen's boots.

All several sizes too small for Tom. There was a mannequin of Rescue Annie resting on its side. The sad death mask face with its eyes forever closed. The mouth agape. He moved the doll and saw a cardboard box. He pulled it out and opened it up. Old VHS tapes. Pornography, mostly. A couple of Chuck Norris films. Several issues of a magazine called *Thick*, two copies of *Slap*. One of *Yes*. Tom binned the doll, the tapes, the magazines.

He went across the landing to the bathroom. It was small and smelled of bleach. The toilet bowl was pink and a dirty crack ran up the side of the rim. Hairs were stuck on the underside of the plastic seat. The sink was the colour of avocado. White blobs of toothpaste had hardened around the taps. He washed his face and hands and went back to his room. He took off his shoes and socks and lay down on the bed. He could see smears of snot on the wall. He heard a door slam shut. There was the sound of vomiting and then low, torpid voices. Another door opened somewhere. Springs squeaked as someone fell on to a bed. Then: there was nothing.

Tom switched off the light, curled up under his covers, and closed his eyes. He saw the unsteady, clumsy footsteps of Galloway and Tucker. The splashes of white paint on their chests. Blood dripping from their wounds. Braudy lying face down in the snow. Drunk and ready to die.

Tom was awoken by the sound of bottles being dropped into one of the wheelie bins in the back yard. He saw Ken walking back indoors. More snow had gathered on the window panes. The light was soft. He got up, dressed, and collected the bin bags filled with Tucker's things. He dropped the bags on the workbench in the office.

In the bar, Cora read an old magazine by the fire. She wore

a Shetland jumper and a tweed skirt. Thick black tights. He sat down on the pool table.

'I have something for you,' he said.

'What?'

He handed her Tucker's pouch of tobacco. She smiled.

'Warmer now?' she asked. 'No tingling? Blisters?'

'I can nearly feel my toes again.'

'Did you stay up for long?'

'Nah. You?'

'Out like a light.'

She straightened out her skirt. 'Were those towels okay?'

'Good. Soft.'

She tried to smile. 'How's your new room?'

Tom shifted and the pool table creaked. 'How to put it...'

'Dirty?'

'There's that,' he said. 'And – well. It's Tucker's stuff. His clothes. And the corsets.'

'They're not mine.'

'I didn't think they were.'

'Tucker used to steal underwear.' She reddened slightly. 'Never told Frank.'

Tom looked up at the leaking ceiling. He could see plastic pipes through the points where the plaster had fallen away.

'I found all sorts. Hats. Shoes. Some of his magazines.'

'Ah, his precious magazines. There was one called... what was it? Chunk? Something like that?'

'*Thick.*'

She smiled. 'That's the one. The sister magazine of *Thin.*'

'That right?'

'*Thick* and *Thin. Hairy* and *Bald.* You get the idea. Tucker worked on a few of them.'

'As what? A photographer?'

She shook her head. 'He used to go and find the girls. Picked them off the streets. No questions asked. Paid them a fiver a session.'

'That all?'

'They were desperate.' Cora wiped a faint trace of lipstick from the side of her coffee cup. Tom heard a door open and slam shut.

'They talk about starting that all up again,' she continued. 'Magazines. Clubs. My dad used to bounce for Frank. On one of his places in Leeds. Had some sort of stupid name. Legs. Wings. Some shit like that. All closed now. Nearly put Frank out of business.'

'Your dad still alive?'

She smiled. 'No.'

'What about your mum?'

'We should talk about something else.'

The door to the office opened. Ken stood there. His eyes were bloodshot. He was pale and looked exhausted.

'What are these bin bags doing on the workbench?' he asked.

'I thought Braudy might want to go through them. For keepsakes.'

'Keepsakes? Bollocks.'

'There are clothes too.'

'Chuck it. I want it gone.'

'Okay.'

Ken looked at his watch. 'First off, come with me.'

Tom put his cup down and followed Ken out to the safe room. The metal door was open. Tom could smell lemons. The floor was wet. The white walls were scuffed and dirty. The plastic sheeting had been stuffed into bin bags. The tap in the corner of the room dripped slowly. A thin trickle of red-brown water flowed into the grating in the centre of the room. Pieces of the chairs were neatly stacked near the door and the leftover nails and screws had been gathered in an old coffee jar.

'Told you to watch yourself with her, Tom.'

'We were just talking.'

'She gave you those towels didn't she?'

'She was just being kind.'

'Those were new fucking towels,' said Ken.

'So what?'

'Remember what I said, Tom. You might have saved Braudy but I've got my beady eye on you.'

Tom sighed and said, 'What do you need me to do?'

He looked around the room and picked up a bottle of sugar soap. 'These walls need a wash down.'

'How thorough?'

'So they're bloody clean, dipshit,' he said. 'A cup of sugar soap per wall should be enough.' Ken handed Tom a red bucket and a pair of pink Marigolds. Tom put on the gloves and found a cloth on one of the trestle tables in the corner. Ken gathered up the bin bags and chair legs and carried them out to the corridor.

CHAPTER EIGHTEEN

THE POWER HAD cut out again. Tom lit a candle. He opened Tucker's copy of *Treasure Island* and took out the photo of Stephanie. The corners of the print were dog-eared and the image was scratched. He looked at it for a while and then put it down on the table. He started to read the book. Someone coughed in another room. He looked up at the wallpaper. The swooping planes. He went back to the book. There were a few numbers written in the margins. A few names he couldn't quite make out. After a while, Tom put the book down and watched the snow. It fell like ash.

In the morning, he woke up and checked his watch. It was before nine. He could smell stale sweat. He swung his legs out of bed and put his feet down on the sticky carpet. The electricity was still off. He went to the bathroom across the corridor. He undressed and stepped into the shower cubicle. Mould stained the white tiles. The stainless steel taps were stiff and covered with limescale. There was a pair of wet orange underpants near the plughole. He picked them up and put them in the sink. He stepped back into the shower. The water was cold.

He heard a knock at the door.

'It's locked,' said Tom.

Someone tried the handle.

'I'll just be a minute.'

The door was kicked and then there was silence. Tom

turned off the shower and wrapped the towel around his waist. He opened the door and noticed a dent where it had been kicked. He looked down the landing.

He got dressed and went downstairs. Ken was at the bar. He was dressed in jogging bottoms, a T-shirt, and a navy-blue blazer. He was eating Corn Flakes and reading an issue of *Thick*.

Tom sat down near the fire. Damp plaster had crumbled on to the pool table.

'The bucket's filling up again,' said Tom.

'The water's coming from Frank's bathroom. Leaking u-bend. I glued it up. Should be sorted now.'

'What about the ceiling.'

'It's fucked. Have to wait for it to dry out before I can do anything.'

'You didn't just knock on the bathroom door, did you?'

'Must have been Braudy.'

'How are his hands?'

'Fucked,' he said. 'Here. This is interesting.' Ken held up the magazine for Tom to see. There was a picture of a naked woman on the edge of a stage. Ten pound notes in her purple g-string. Smiling. Legs spread. Cupping her breasts. 'Says here thirty per cent of women have worked in the sex trade. Thirty per cent.'

'Is that true?'

'Woman here is a teacher. Makes extra money by stripping. Rents half-hour spots at a local club. She keeps the tips. Might make for an awkward parents' evening every now and then but it's a good idea, isn't it?'

'Good idea for who?'

'The club. The women. The punters.'

Ken finished his Corn Flakes. Tom looked at the front of the magazine. There was a woman dressed as an elf. She sat on a man in a Santa outfit. Both of them looked surprised. He saw the date of the issue. November 1995. Christmas edition.

'Is there any coffee?'

'Power's off. Might be some Corn Flakes. The sweepings.'

'I'll see what I can find.'

'Take a torch.'

In the office, Tom searched one of the desks and found tools and batteries. There was a small torch hidden beneath a hank of red wool. He checked it worked, and walked down the dark corridor to the kitchen. It was murky and the fridges were silent. Tom opened the cupboards. He found a couple of tins of soup. A can of mincemeat. There was nothing else in the fridges except Ken's socks and the out-of-date yoghurt. He returned to the bar.

Ken looked up from *Thick*. 'Find anything?'

'Some cans.'

'How many?'

'Three or four.'

'Get your coat on,' said Ken, putting his magazine down. 'We'll get some more boxes in from the cellar.'

In the yard, they passed Frank's truck. It was completely covered with snow. They reached the side of the building. Ken unlocked the metal door, opened it, and climbed down the wooden stairs. Tom went down into the cellar after him. The steps creaked. He could smell clay and stagnant water. Ken gently kicked each beer barrel with the side of his foot.

'Getting low on the porter,' he said.

Tom touched the shelf and saw Frank's pickling jars. The faint light of Ken's torch made the eggs look like specimens in a laboratory. Ken went over to the metal cabinet and checked it was locked. He paused for a moment and listened. There was a gentle humming sound. He went over to the switch and flicked it on. The bulb lit up and Ken smiled.

'There I was worrying we'd have to have a cold lunch.' He bent down and moved some of the cardboard boxes out of the way. Behind them there were crates of supplies. Tinned food. Cream crackers, noodles. Eight cartons of UHT milk. Three more packets of coffee.

'This is the last of it,' said Ken. 'Take the milk and the coffee.'

Tom reached down and lifted the crate on to his shoulder. He took it outside. Ken came up from the cellar carrying the two other crates of food. He put them down and locked the hatch.

Back in the kitchen they put the crates on the table. Ken took a pen and a piece of paper from his blazer pocket and listed the items in the crates. When everything was accounted for, he prepared a lunch of minestrone soup and crackers.

They ate in the bar. Ken slurped his soup, spilling some of it on to the table. Tom heard a hacking cough from upstairs. Ken crumbled up a cracker and sprinkled it into his soup. 'Thing with Frank is that he doesn't stop. Can't switch off. All this drives him fucking nuts. Last holiday he had was a year ago.'

'Where did he go?'

'Sweden. It was Mandy's idea. Wanted to go on an Abba tour or some shit like that.'

'Does Frank even like Abba?'

'I'm amazed you even have to ask. Nah. He was bored out of his mind. Kept phoning us to check we hadn't fucked up.'

'Did you?'

'Not massively, no.'

After eating, Tom read while Ken worked on a matchstick model. He carefully cut off the match heads and put them in a jar. Then, with great care, he glued the matchsticks together, blowing on them to dry the glue more quickly. It looked as if he would crush the model, through clumsiness or strength, but his touch was sure, precise.

'What's that you're building?'

'A cathedral.'

'Which bit?'

'A narthex,' said Ken. 'I'll start on the apse next.'

'That take long?'

'Yep.'

'Frank said you built another model. A while back.'

'Couple of years ago.'

'What happened to it?'

'Chucked it before Tucker got a chance to burn it.' He held the model up to the light. 'Might keep this one. See how well it turns out.'

'It looks good.'

'You don't even know what a narthex is, do you?'

'No.'

'Then how do you know it looks good?'

'Just does,' said Tom.

It drizzled in the afternoon but at night the temperature dropped again. In the morning, Tom went to the laundry room. The green wallpaper had started to peel away from the plasterboard. The worn carpet was marked with spots of bleach. He saw the red jumper Braudy had worn. It was hanging upside-down over a radiator. The clothes horse was draped with underpants. Some were of his size. He wondered if they had once belonged to him. Even if they were his, it seemed like it would be strange to reclaim them after they had been worn by someone else. There was a shelf filled with sample bottles of washing detergents and fabric conditioners. Tom chose one called Summer Breeze. The washing machine was an old top loader. A brown plastic lid. Chunky controls. He put in his muddy clothes, his damp T-shirts. The towels Cora had given him. Once the wash was done, he took the clothes through to the bar. He laid out his smalls on the fireguard and draped his other clothes over the radiators. He stoked the fire and made himself some strong coffee. Ken's matchstick model was drying on two sheets of newspaper. Blobs of glue had defaced the photo on the back page. It was the same edition Galloway had read.

After midday, Ken came in, whistling to himself. 'Any sign of Braudy?'

'No.'

'He's not in his room,' said Ken.

'Bathroom?'

'Not there either. Stupid bugger.' He poured himself a cup of coffee and took a sip. 'Jesus. How much did you put in?'

'Four spoonfuls.'

'Four? Think, lad. We need the coffee to last.' Ken took another sip and pulled a face. He put four spoonfuls of sugar into his coffee and stirred it.

'Aren't we running out of sugar too?' asked Tom.

'Don't get cocky,' he replied.

At one, they put on their coats and boots. Ken started clearing the snow around the store, and sent Tom to clear the back of the building. He walked past the fishing boat. It was covered with ice. Water dripped from the holes in the hull. Weeds poked out near the base of the metal climbing frame. Steam rose slowly from the vent in the wall. He started to dig a path. He saw the abandoned bathtub lying on its side. The strands of dirty hair had frozen stiff.

When he had reached the oil tank, he went to find Ken. He was sitting on the stone wall near the entrance. There was a sack of grit at his feet. He hawked up phlegm as Tom approached.

'Feel a bit warmer to you?' asked Ken.

'A bit.'

'You finished?'

'Think so.'

'Throw down some grit and call it a day.'

Tom picked up the sack. Inside it, there was a small plastic margarine tub. He used it to scoop out the grit. When he was finished, he returned indoors. In the bar, he picked up some of his dry clothes from the radiators and went upstairs. On the landing, Cora stepped out of her bedroom. She put her finger to her lips and he went over to her. There was a sweet smell. Something between rose petals and sweat. He looked over her shoulder and saw a single canopy bed sitting against the back wall. Plastic ivy wound up the bedposts. The front windows were open and the curtains stirred in the cold breeze.

'I heard someone creeping about,' she said.

Tom looked back at his room. The door was half-open. They heard Braudy's voice. He was talking to himself.

'Wait for a while,' said Cora. 'Or get Ken. Or Frank.'

'I better go and speak with him. Try and sort things out.'

'What's the point? He's drunk.'

'Let me try.' He crossed the landing and stood outside his bedroom. He looked back at Cora and pushed open the door. Braudy was sitting on the bed and had lit the candle on the bedside table. He wore a red body warmer over his cotton pyjamas. The tip of his nose and chin were red and blistered. He balanced a silver hip flask between his knees and peeked under the bandages that covered his hands.

He looked up and said, 'Where you been?'

'Gritting.'

He wiped drool from his chin and started to unwind the dressings. The skin on his fingers was black. The nails were grey and looked as if they were about to fall away from the flesh. He looked around the room. 'What'd you fucking do with Chloe?'

'Who?'

'Chloe. Picture of the bird with her arse in the air. Where is it?'

'I threw it out.'

Braudy took a sip from the flask. 'What else did you get rid of?'

'Rubbish, mostly.'

Braudy burped and held his hand over his mouth for a couple of seconds. 'Where did you put Tucker's magazines?'

'I threw them out too.' Tom moved into the room.

'How am I meant to remember him?'

'I'm sorry. I didn't realise.'

Braudy rested his head on the wall. An uneven smile darkened his expression. He swigged from the flask. 'It's a shame you got rid of old Chloe.'

'Why?'

'Didn't you see the resemblance?'

'Which bit?'

'Her face,' he said. 'Her fucking eyes.'

'No.'

'No? Chloe was a relative of mine. Cousin. Tucker spotted her when she was sixteen. Found her drinking in a park. Took her back to the studio.' Braudy held out the hip flask to Tom, who shook his head. 'She was good looking. Don't you think?'

'I didn't see.'

'Lily white, aren't you?'

'What's this about?'

Braudy waved a hand vaguely and said, 'You can't fool me, Tom.'

'No?'

'You're hiding something, you sly bastard.' He drained the hip flask. 'All that shit about your girlfriend. Dying in a car accident.'

'That's what happened.'

'You're lying, Tom.'

'Get out of my room.'

'That photo you kept in your wallet. Tucker told me.' Braudy closed one eye and looked down the neck of the flask.

'You knew about it?'

'Looked like this, didn't it?' He pulled out the photo of Stephanie from the pocket of his body warmer. 'When Tucker first showed it me, I didn't know what it meant. Things have changed though, haven't they?'

'Give it back.'

Braudy looked at the picture. 'Did you come on her tits?'

'Please.'

'She take it up the arse?'

'Why don't we try to straighten this out?'

'For who? You? Or me?'

'Everyone.'

Braudy reached over to the candle and held the photograph over the flame. It burned quickly. Tom lunged forward and Braudy swung a heavy left towards the side of Tom's head, just grazing his jaw. Tom threw a fist and caught Braudy on the nose. Blood squirted out and he sat down heavily on the bed. Tom stood there, holding his fists up, ready for more.

Braudy shouted out and came back at Tom, striking him on the eye and chin. Tom hit back but Braudy kept coming, swinging his fists wildly. Some of the blows landed and Tom guarded his head with his arms and retreated back into the corridor. In one, slow movement, Braudy took another swing at him and missed. His fist smashed into the wall. There was a crack. He shouted from the pain and held his hand under his armpit. Blood covered his nose and chin.

Tom turned to see Frank standing next to the old chest of drawers. His skin was loose and grey and looked like it was moulded from putty. Grey shadows circled his eyes. He wore old flannel pyjamas. His kimono was wrapped around him, the cord around his waist pulled tight. He held a pistol in his right hand. Cora looked on from her bedroom.

'Step away, Tom,' said Frank.

Braudy shook his head. He fell to the floor and vomited on to the carpet.

'Did he hurt you?'

'I think he broke his hand,' said Tom.

'On you?'

'The wall.'

Braudy was curled up on the floor, sobbing. Frank turned to Cora and waved her away. She closed the door.

Tom helped Braudy to his feet and cleaned him up in the bathroom. Frank helped to drag Braudy down the landing towards his bedroom. There were piles of old newspapers, full ashtrays. Faded posters of 1950s science fiction films. There were several bottles of whisky and vodka lined up on the window sill. Some were full. Some were empty. Braudy lay down on his bed, eyes red, cheeks damp from tears. Frank left, coughing into a handkerchief. Tom followed him out, switched off the light, and closed the door.

CHAPTER NINETEEN

T OM WENT DOWN the stairs and into the bar. Ken had his feet up and was drinking brandy from a chipped glass. He was watching a small spider crawl over the matchstick model of the cathedral. The spider stopped for a moment before carrying on across the table. Tom had a drink of water and sat down at the counter. His hands were shaking. He looked out of the window. It had started to drizzle.

Ken swirled his brandy around and said, 'Did Braudy do that to you?'

'What?'

'Your left eye.'

Tom touched it and realised he was bleeding. He took a piece of kitchen paper and dabbed at the cut. There wasn't much blood.

'You should drink something stronger.'

Tom held out his glass and Ken filled it with brandy.

The specials board had been wiped clean. A brush and a small tin of blackboard paint was sitting on the pool table. The phone started to ring. Tom and Ken looked at one another, both surprised by the shrillness of the sound.

'Do you want me to answer it?' asked Tom.

Ken shook his head slowly.

'It might be help.'

'Like what?'

'I dunno. Fire brigade. Mountain rescue.'

'We don't need rescuing,' said Ken. 'Leave it.'

There were twelve further rings before it stopped. Tom went behind the bar and picked up the phone. He checked the last number called. 'Number withheld,' he said.

'Probably PPI or something.'

Tom sniffed the brandy. 'Or – or it could have been the phone company. Testing the line.'

'How would that work if we didn't answer it?'

'Well. They see if a – a circuit is – you know. Completed. A line test.'

Ken grunted and reached over to the model of the cathedral. He pushed it aside and scratched at a small spot of glue which had hardened overnight. The phone started to ring again. It seemed louder than before. Ken rubbed his forehead. He blew out his cheeks and said, 'Go ahead. Answer it, Tom.'

'Sure?'

'Tell them we're busy. Or tell them to fuck off. Up to you.'

Tom picked up the phone and said, 'Hello?'

He listened for a moment, and heard soft crackles. Electronic squeaks and whines.

'Who is it?' asked Ken.

'It's just static. Oh. Hold on. Hold on.' Tom heard a voice. There were parts of words. He couldn't make it out. The phone went dead. He dialled to find the last number called.

'Who is it?'

'Same again,' he said.

Ken groaned. 'It better not be fucking Wayne.'

Tom finished his brandy and Ken refilled the glass.

'Make this one last,' he said.

Tom heard a creak of floorboards above. Slow, heavy

footsteps paused halfway down the stairs. He gripped his glass and heard a door close. Ken looked straight ahead at the bottles of whisky and brandy. He picked up a cloth wrapped around one of the pumps and wiped the counter. Frank came into the room, smelling of Olbas oil. He pushed out two aspirin from a half-empty blister pack. He popped the pills in his mouth, crunched them up, and swallowed. He swilled out his mouth with some water.

'Feeling worse, Frank?' asked Ken.

'There any lemon?'

'There's a lime in the fridge.'

'No lemon?'

'No.'

Frank took down a bottle of whisky from the bar and boiled the kettle and squeezed lime juice into a pint glass. He added four sachets of sugar, whisky, and hot water. He gave the mixture a stir and knocked it back in one.

'Let's have a look at what Braudy did.' His voice was heavy with catarrh. He reached out and touched the cut on Tom's eye.

'Leave it,' said Tom, pushing Frank's hand away.

'Don't be such a pussy. That's barely a scratch.'

The cut had reopened. Tom dabbed at it with the back of his hand. He got some kitchen paper and held it against the wound.

'Someone's tried to call,' said Ken.

'Now? For fuck sake.' Frank sighed. 'Who was it?'

'It was a bad line,' said Tom.

'Probably wrong number then.'

'Or PPI.'

'Could be different people,' replied Tom.

'No cunt comes up here,' said Frank.

'Galloway did.'

'Wayne might.'

'Shut up,' said Frank. The whites of his eyes were a faded yellow. The lids red and sore. Frank pulled off a couple more sheets of kitchen paper and blew his nose. The phone rang again.

'Was it always that loud?' asked Frank. He coughed up some phlegm and spat it into the fire. The ringing stopped after a minute.

Ken sat back in his chair, and fiddled with the lump of hardened glue on the table. 'What if it is Wayne?'

'Don't need you panicking today.'

'I'm not panicking,' said Ken. 'I'm being practical.'

'He'll be up here whatever we do. Sent Galloway here, didn't he?' Frank glanced at the front yard. 'Not much we can do to stop him.'

'Can we delay him?' asked Ken. 'Tell him we've all got fucking ebola or something.'

Frank put his hands flat on the bar. He looked straight ahead and furrowed his brow. Ken was about to say something but Frank put his hand up for silence. He pinched his bottom lip. Wheezing as he breathed.

After a minute, Frank said, 'If I ignore him he'll drop in here unannounced. Maybe in a good mood. Maybe not.'

'It might not be Wayne,' said Tom.

'We play it right, Wayne can come up here thinking we're going to help him.'

'Doesn't matter what he thinks,' said Ken. 'It's what he sees that'll fuck us.'

'I'll make up some story. Say that Galloway ran out on him.

Tell him he had a piece of skirt with him. A piece of skirt and a bag of money.'

'Wayne won't fall for that,' said Tom.

Frank's expression darkened. 'How long have you known Wayne for? Longer than me?'

'No.'

'Right. Button it, then.' Frank carried a stool behind the bar and over to the phone. 'We may as well get this out of the bloody way.'

'Let's think about this, Frank.'

Frank cradled the phone between his shoulder and chin. He started to dial. He smiled when the phone was answered. 'Wayne? It's Frank. Yeah. A lot of snow. A lot. We've been stuck here. Not resorted to cannibalism yet. Yeah. Too cold for snowmen. Too cold for sledging.'

Ken picked up the pieces of his model cathedral and turned it about in the light. He ran a dirty thumbnail down the rough edges and scratched away at the excess glue.

Frank curled the telephone cord around his fingers. A strange smile worked its way on to his lips. He got off his stool and took a faded postcard from the cork board. He read the back of it. Ken put his chin on his chest and scratched harder at the glue on the matchstick model. Some of the wood came away and went beneath his thumbnail. He winced and pulled out a splinter.

Tom dabbed at the cut on his eye with scrunched-up kitchen paper. He touched his ear and jaw, wondering if he'd been hit hard enough to bruise. The fight was already hazy in his memory. Dreamlike. He saw Frank's knuckles had whitened from gripping the phone. Tom wanted to take it off him. Or pull the cord out. Smash the phone into little pieces.

They both heard Frank swear. Wayne was a cunt. Wayne was a snake. Frank was struggling to get his words out. Beads of sweat formed on his upper lip. He wiped at his forehead with his handkerchief and poured himself some more whisky. Ken got out of his seat and moved around the side of the bar. His steps were unsteady. He waved at Frank and mouthed words at him. Cut. Stop. He drew his finger across his throat but Frank only turned his back on him.

'Galloway isn't here. Never was. You're wasting your time, Wayne,' said Frank. 'Don't call me a prick. I'm not – I'm not a fucking prick. Wayne? Hello? Shit.'

Frank looked at the phone and then hung up. He took out a cigarette and lit it.

Ken attempted to smile. 'When's he coming?'

'Once the roads are clear.'

Tom looked out of the window. The fine rain continued to fall. A light mist hung over the hills. Night was not far away. Frank took another drag and got smoke in his eyes. He blinked. 'We'll send him off on a wild goose chase. Buy us some time to work out how to get rid of him. Once and for all.'

Ken ran a hand across the top of his head. 'When he finds out what you did to Galloway—'

'What I did? What I did? You were there too, you little bastard.'

'Frank.'

'You sitting yourself out of the game, Ken? Thought we'd moved on from that.'

'We have.'

'Right then.'

Ken tried to smile. 'I guess there's still the snow.'

'Fucking hell. At last. Some positive thinking. We still have the fucking snow.'

The phone started to ring again. Frank finished his hot toddy, threw the lime into the fire, and left the room.

Tom went upstairs. The landing still smelled of vomit. Someone had laid down towels to soak up the stains. He went into his bedroom. There was a mark in the plaster where Braudy had punched the wall. The candle was out. The ashes of Stephanie's photo were scattered over the carpet. He switched on the bedside lamp and sniffed. He could smell something. Thinking that Braudy had vomited somewhere, he checked the bin. The bedside table. The wardrobe. Beneath his bed. He couldn't see anything. He collected fresh bed linen from the cupboard downstairs and changed his bed. Tired and cold, he got undressed. He opened up Treasure Island and discovered that Part III was missing. He read on regardless, until he could barely keep his eyes open. Yawning, he looked at the dusty cobwebs in the corner of the room.

There was a knock on the door.

'Yeah?'

'It's Cora.'

'Hang on.' Tom put on his trousers. 'Okay.'

Cora came into the room. She was wearing tartan pyjamas and a T-shirt printed with a wrinkled image of Debbie Harry. She held a hot water bottle in her right hand.

'You doing okay?'

Tom sat down on his bed. 'Not bad.'

'This room smells funny.'

'Braudy,' he said. 'And Tucker, I suppose.'

She sat down on the bed and pushed down on the mattress.

Tom smoothed out the creased duvet cover. 'I used to sleep less before I came here,' he said.

'Frank hates sleep. He finds it slovenly. He finds me slovenly.'

'What else is there to do?'

Cora stood and opened the wardrobe. She searched through Tucker's suits and took out the corsets and held them up.

'Mandy's?'

'Possibly,' she said, putting the corsets back.

Tom heard a noise. He looked at the door, expecting to see someone. Cora looked down the corridor. There was another noise.

'It's just Ken,' said Cora. 'Talking in his sleep.'

'What do we say if Frank comes in?'

'You offered to show me your etchings?'

'Don't kid around, Cora,' he said.

'Relax, Tom. We're just talking.'

Tom lowered his voice. 'Do you still want to leave?'

'It's better than staying here and dying. Waiting for Wayne to turn up.'

'So what do we do? Steal the truck? Go on the run?'

'Why not?'

'How?' he asked.

'I can get hold of Ken's set of truck keys. He's lost them before. He can lose them again.'

There was a noise. He listened. Cora moved back towards the door. Tom could hear the water gurgle in the radiators.

'We need to leave,' she said. 'And you need to face up to what's happened. With what you've been through up here. With Stephanie—'

'Cora—'

Cora put down her hot water bottle on the bed. She knelt down, looked him in the eyes, and said, 'We can't hide here any more, Tom.'

'I still think about her, you know. Stephanie. What happened.'

'Why haven't you told me the truth, Tom?'

He held his hand over his mouth for a moment.

'Who killed her, Tom?'

'I came home to find she'd cut her wrists with a piece of broken glass.' He started to cry. 'She was so pale. There was blood everywhere. I couldn't find a pulse. And there was no note.'

'Tom—'

'I was so sure she was getting better. We'd bought a Christmas tree. Bought presents. Written cards to her fucking family,' he said.

'It wasn't your fault, Tom.'

'I can't even remember the last time I told her I loved her.'

Cora touched his shoulder and he dried his eyes on the duvet cover. The lights flickered. Tom heard another shout from Ken's room. He could smell rubber and a light fragrance of apples.

'You have to try and carry on,' she said. 'You need to leave here. We both do.'

'And then what? They catch and kill us?'

'We have to try, Tom. We have to.'

'I don't know if I can.'

'I'm not going to wait for you to make your mind up.'

Cora stood up, looked at him for a moment and then left the room.

He reached over to the window and wiped at the

condensation on the glass. The rain was heavier than before. In places, the grit had thinned the snow out into a translucent brown slush. It would freeze over in the night, but the thaw would begin anew by morning.

CHAPTER TWENTY

TOM WENT FOR a walk. It was very cold, made worse by the bitter wind. He followed a vague path that ran parallel with the road. The snow was still thick in places and a layer of ice capped the drystone wall. Blades of tall grass poked through the surface of the wet snow still covering the fields. He listened to meltwater trickling into gullies. The chirrup and squawk of birds. He reached the grass verge where Gary had dropped him off. He stood on the dirty snow. Ice had preserved old tyre tracks where other cars had stopped and turned back. He could not decide if Gary had helped him by bringing him here or if he had merely delayed his death. It did not seem to matter. His friend had paid a dreadful price trying to save his life. The only thing Tom could do now was to try and escape with Cora. He did not know where they could go. Both Wayne and Frank would come after them. United by the draw of bounty and the need for revenge.

He heard a noise and looked back at the Bothy. He saw a figure standing at the front door, shouting. It was Frank. There was anger in his voice. Frustration. Tom waved at him and turned back.

Frank shouted, 'Come on, Tom. Stop dawdling.'

Tom waved again but did not walk any faster. He reached the front yard. Ice covered the truck. The stuffed animal tied to the radiator wore a small cap of snow. Water dripped from its feet.

Frank was by the fireplace.

'Weren't you going to cut more wood this morning?'

'Thought we had enough.'

He held up the basket. It was half full.

'I'll get more now,' said Tom.

'Get it later.' Frank kneeled down and stacked kindling in the fireplace. His clothes were marked with soot and ash. 'Ken says we're getting short of oil.'

'It's warming up.'

'So?'

'You'll be able to get the truck out. Get some more supplies. More food.'

Frank struck a match and threw it on to the wood. He threw on some firewood and twisted a page of newspaper into a long taper. He stuffed it between the logs and stepped back.

'Tried to get Braudy to apologise to you.'

'I don't want an apology,' said Tom, getting himself a drink.

'Why not?'

'What good would it do?'

There were bits of broken bottle on the floor. Tom picked up a dustpan and brush and swept up the glass.

'He's still upstairs,' said Frank. 'Trying to sleep off his hangover. Getting rid of the shakes.'

'Jesus.'

'Shame we have no fresh eggs. Take them raw. A bit of Worcestershire sauce. Ever try that, Tom?'

'Yeah.'

'Works, doesn't it?'

'Not in the way you might expect,' said Tom. 'What about pickled eggs?'

'I'm not opening a new jar just because he can't handle his liquor.' Frank wiped newsprint off his hands and added a handful of kindling on to the logs. He struck a match. He lit the end of the tapered newspaper and threw on some twigs. White smoke rose up but there were no flames.

'We got any moss, Tom? That's good for starting fires.' Frank lit another match and held it against the kindling. He flicked the match into the fireplace and sat back as the single flame dwindled and died. The newspaper smouldered.

'Does Ken use lighter fluid? Diesel?'

'No.'

'He must have used a – uh – an accelerant.' Frank knelt down again and lit another piece of kindling. He tucked it in between the logs and smiled when he saw smoke.

'Think you put on too much wood,' said Tom.

'Don't you bloody start.' Frank blew gently on to the kindling. The flames went out. He lit another piece of torn newspaper. Flames blackened the pictures, the print.

He picked up a brass poker. He jabbed at the logs and brushed at the soot on the hearth. 'Try and get the fire going, Tom. I'll go and see if I can find some sodding lighter fluid.'

Tom was left alone. He heard someone move around upstairs. Maybe Braudy returning to his room. Maybe Ken getting up. He sat down and pulled out the logs from the fire. In the centre of the fireplace, he arranged some fresh kindling and lit it. He blew on the flame a few times and rested a log on the fire. The splintered tips of wood blackened. He remembered the trick he had seen Cora perform to get the fire going. He picked up a sheet of newspaper from the basket and held a double page over the mouth of the fireplace. The strength of the updraft took him by surprise and the newspaper was sucked into the chimney. He quickly pulled the paper out, screwed it up, and tossed it on to the burning logs.

Tom stepped back and watched the orange flames. He went back to his bedroom, opened the wardrobe, and took out Tucker's clothes and the corsets. He put them in the black bin bag. After spraying the room with air freshener he lay down on his bed.

CHAPTER TWENTY-ONE

T OM SHAVED WITH a blunt razor, and nicked himself
twice on the chin. He pressed pink toilet paper over the
cuts, and looked for a styptic pencil in the medicine cabinet.
There was an unopened tube of Deep Heat, some Vaseline. A
few bottles of pills. The expiry dates were faded. He wrapped
himself in his towel, returned to his room, and sat down on
his bed. He watched the shadows shorten and the sunlight
spread over the hills and fields. Water dripped from the roof.

Outside, birds pecked at the ground. Their eyes were bright
in the cold light. He listened to people move about the house.
Slammed doors. Ripples of bitter laughter. Braudy came down
the landing, singing. A religious song. A half-remembered
hymn. Tom tensed and waited for the knock. It did not come.
Braudy resumed his singing and went downstairs.

Tom stepped over the stain on the landing carpet where
Braudy had vomited. He raised his fist and knocked on Cora's
door. He listened and then knocked again. There was no
answer.

In the office, Ken was sitting on a workbench eating cold
beans from a can. Tupperware boxes full of bullets were laid
out on the workbenches and desks. Each box was labelled with
embossing tape. Steel cap. Hollow point. Boat tail. Frangible.
The mended trophies sat on the table at the back. The figure
without the head looked like he was falling backwards. Tom
heard Frank and Braudy speaking in the bar. They both

sounded angry. Ken ate another forkful of beans and chewed thoughtfully. He scraped at his teeth and ate the orange morsel on the end of his forefinger. 'What did you do to your face?'

'Shaving.'

'Still haven't got the hang of it?' Ken wiped some tomato sauce from his lips. He put the can down and wiped his hands on his trousers. 'Come on. We've got a few things to do. Need to check the truck.'

'Why?'

'Because it's the first Thursday of the month. And the cold can fuck with the tyre pressure. Amongst other things.'

Tom put on a coat and red wellingtons. Ken lifted up a large holdall, a battered shoe box, and a red, scuffed foot pump. They went out to the front yard. A light rain fell. Ken noticed the teddy bear attached to the front of the truck was coming loose. He knelt down and tightened the metal wire holding the bear in place. Moving around to the front tyre, he unscrewed the dust cap, and handed it to Tom. He attached the foot pump and checked the tyre pressure. He disengaged the pump and held out his hand. Tom gave him the dust cap. Ken screwed it back on. With a grunt he got to his feet. They checked the other tyres. Little dimples had appeared in the snow where the rain had fallen. Ken knelt down in front of the headlights, prising the plastic covering away from the clips with a rusty screwdriver. He handed the cover to Tom and said, 'Pass me that box. Over there.'

'This one?'

'Yeah.'

Tom handed him the shoebox. It contained bulbs. All different sizes. Ken selected a bulb and screwed it into the fitting.

'You see the truck keys around, Tom?' he asked.

'No. Where did you see them last?'

'They were in this coat. Anything you want to talk to me about?'

'I've not touched them, Ken. Have you told Frank?'

'He's got enough to worry about,' he said. 'Hand me another bulb.'

They checked the lights were working and then walked around to the cellar. Ken wiped wet snow from the hatch and brought out a bunch of keys. He unlocked the two padlocks. After lifting the rusting hasps, he opened the metal hatch, and climbed down the stairs. The light came on.

Tom climbed down a couple of steps. He saw dirty puddles on the ground. He could smell wet dirt and mildew. Water marks reached half a metre up the wall. The old mattress was soaked through and stinking. The cardboard boxes in the corner were deformed and soggy. Tom peered inside the boxes. The photo albums were stained with dirt and the pages of the magazines had curled and wrinkled. The jars of pickled eggs still sat on the shelves, unharmed.

Ken put the holdall down and unlocked the metal cabinet in the corner. There was still a little water trapped inside. Standing in a rack, there were two shotguns, and three rifles. A plastic Tesco bag full of pistols and silencers. Tom saw a small box of grenades and three small vials of white powder.

Ken transferred a shotgun, two rifles, and four pistols into the holdall. He locked the cabinet and took the bag off Tom.

'Grab a jar of eggs,' he said.

'Anything else?'

'Just the eggs.'

They went back indoors. Frank was sitting on a barstool drinking a pint of bitter. His face was red and sweat patches showed on his shirt, on his back, around his armpits. There was a sweet smell of raw onions.

Tom placed the jar of eggs behind the bar and sat down on the pool table.

'Have you decided what we're going to tell Wayne yet?' asked Ken.

Frank said, 'We tell him we never saw Galloway.'

'I thought we were going to say we'd seen him with a woman,' said Tom.

'Have you seen the state of Braudy? The daft twat will bugger it up. Better to keep the lie simple.'

Tom picked up the discoloured cue ball. It was cold.

Frank scratched under his armpit, and said, 'So what else do we need to do before Wayne turns up?'

'I've got the weapons.'

'Ammo?'

'All tested,' said Ken.

'Sure?'

'Hundred per cent,' he said, reaching into the holdall. He took out a couple of revolvers. 'I'm going to get a couple of these hidden away. Just in case they decide to get handy.'

'Won't get to that stage,' said Frank. 'It'll be a nice civilised chat over a few beers.'

'And then?'

'Then they'll go home.'

Ken nodded towards Tom. 'How do we explain him to Wayne?'

'Proves Galloway couldn't have got here,' said Frank. 'Galloway is Wayne's best man. If he came here he would have got Tom.'

'Come on, Frank. Wayne's not going to buy that.'

'Oh, he'll buy it all right. Don't you worry.' Frank looked at his watch and said, 'Anyone hungry?'

Ken paused, and then said, 'I could eat.'

'What do we have? Any pies? Chips?'

'Only soup.'

'Perfect.' Frank took out an old envelope and his fountain pen. He hesitated for a moment and then wrote something down. Ken left to prepare the meal.

Tom looked out at the fading light, the grey skies. He tried to picture being somewhere else. Driving away from the Bothy. Cora by his side. Both fighting back the growing awareness that escape would not prolong their lives. That it would only delay their deaths. The fear, the squalor of his life would not change. Nor would its ending.

He fetched some spoons from the white box on the bar. He found the salt cellar hidden behind the coffee machine. He laid out the condiments out on the table near the front door. Frank pulled up a chair and sat down. Then he lit a cigarette. His mouth was downturned. His small eyes were dark and shiny in the low light.

'I could do with a beer,' said Frank.

Tom checked the fridges.

'Two bottles of porter,' said Tom.

'What are they doing in the fridge?'

'Not sure.'

'Give it here. Have one if you want.'

Tom put the bottle down in front of Frank who tapped the lid on the edge of the table. There was a hiss and foam spilled out on to the carpet. He took a swig of the porter and said, 'This stuff shouldn't be cold.'

'Is Braudy joining us for food?'

Frank put out his cigarette and gave a weak smile. 'He's still pissed off. With you. With everything.'

'Still?'

'He has this idea that I should hand you over to Wayne. To keep the peace.'

'Do you agree with him?'

'Braudy's a fool.'

'Is me being here putting you all in danger?'

'I don't want you leaving, Tom.'

'Maybe I should.'

'That would be giving up, Tom. Letting that prick Wayne win. I'm not having that.' Frank picked up an ashtray and gently shook it, as if he was hoping that the ashes might separate out like tea leaves in a cup. 'You spoken to Cora today?'

'No. I haven't.'

Frank put down the ashtray and said, 'She goes quiet sometimes. And when you ask her what the problem is, she says she's scared.' He leaned back in his chair and looked out at the hills. 'When she was in the city she wanted to be in the country. And now she's in the country, she wants to be in the city.'

Ken came in carrying three blue plastic bowls on a tray.

'What have we got here?'

'Tomato soup mixed with mulligatawny.'

'An old favourite.' Frank fiddled with the buttons on his shirt. He picked up a spoon and started to eat. Ken did the same. Tom hesitated. Then he dipped his spoon in and parted the skin that had formed on the surface of the soup. He tasted it. Sweet and spicy.

They were silent for a few minutes. Tom could hear the soft drip of water. The snap of firewood.

'When will Wayne turn up?' asked Tom.

'Tomorrow at the earliest,' said Ken. 'Day after at the latest.'

Frank slurped at his soup and then stirred it. 'You do anything different to this, Ken?'

'No.'

'Tastes hotter than usual.' Frank read the label on the back of the beer bottle. 'Used as a dessert beer this one.'

'Porter's nice with chocolate,' said Ken.

They finished their soup and stacked up their bowls. Frank sat back in his seat and patted his stomach. 'Any coffee?' he asked.

Tom went over to the counter, looked inside the packet of coffee granules, and said, 'This is the last of it.'

'There's no more?'

'None.'

'Make half a pot. Shouldn't be too weak then,' said Ken.

Frank picked up a newspaper. He rested his elbow on the fold and started to read. Tom tipped the coffee into the machine, filled it with water, and then switched it on. There was a smell of burning. Something hissed and gobbets of coffee dripped into the glass carafe.

Ken resumed work on his matchstick cathedral. He dropped one of the matchsticks and reached down and re-trieved it. He wiped off the fluff that had stuck to the glue and tried to attach the stick again. His fingers trembled.

Frank held up his newspaper and laughed, 'Listen to this. Says here that eating too much meat is worse than smoking.'

'What kind of meat?' asked Ken.

'Red meat. Bacon. All that processed stuff. Salami.'

Frank stood up and took out the last bottle of porter from the fridge.

'What did you used to eat, Tom? Before you came here?'

'Girlfriend made a lot of pasta.'

'Pizzas?'

'Turkish pizzas,' said Tom.

'They have meat on them?'

'Yeah.'

'There you go. Cancer,' said Frank.

Tom took the bowls through to the kitchen and put them in the sink. Ken came in with a few glasses. He put them down on the counter and rinsed out the empty soup cans. He dropped them in the bin and sat down at the table. Tom filled the sink with warm water and washed the plastic bowls and the spoons. The glasses on the counter were coated with furry white mould.

'Found those behind one of the curtains,' said Ken.

Tom filled each glass with water and washing-up liquid. The mould floated to the surface.

'They've probably been there all winter.'

Tom wiped at the glasses with the cloth. 'I might soak them.'

'Wise,' replied Ken.

'How do you think it'll go when Wayne turns up?'

Ken breathed in deeply and said, 'Our chances are about the same as they always are. Fair to middling.'

Tom heard someone move around upstairs. Slow, uncertain footsteps. Ken left the room and Tom squeezed out the cloth. He draped it over the side of the sink to dry and listened to mice scratching in the walls.

It was dark when he woke up. The landing light shone through the cracks in the door and the key hole. He could hear Ken snoring. Noises in the yard. The clatter of rubbish pushed about by the breeze. The haunted cry of an animal. Injured or alone. There were footsteps outside his room. Something blocked the light shining through the key hole. Someone was standing outside. There was a gentle tap on the door. He sat up and switched on the light, and hesitated. There was another knock. Harder this time.

'That you, Frank?'

There was no answer. Tom got out of bed, and put on his trousers and a T-shirt. There was another knock.

'Just a minute.'

He tip-toed across the room and opened the door. Braudy was standing there, wearing an olive jacket, jeans, hiking boots. He had taken off his bandages and held a gun in his right hand. 'We're going,' he said.

CHAPTER TWENTY-TWO

B RAUDY GRABBED TOM'S throat with his frostbit-
ten fingers and pushed the gun under his chin. His eyes
were bright and steady. Ken's door was half-open. There was
a strong smell of sweat and aftershave. They could hear him
snoring.

'Where are we going?' asked Tom.

'Outside.'

'I've got no shoes.'

Ken's snoring stopped. He shouted something out and
Tom heard the bedsprings squeak. There was more muttering
and then the snoring resumed.

Braudy pushed Tom towards the stairs. They passed
through the office and entered the bar. It was dark and Tom
felt the gun jab into the small of his back. It surprised him
and he stumbled forward into a stool. It wobbled and fell over.
Braudy grabbed Tom's T-shirt and guided him towards the
door. He was pushed out into the yard. The security lights
clicked on. The ground was wet. Tom could feel cold grit
under his feet. There was still thick snow near the walls.

'Keep walking.'

Tom looked upwards at Cora's room. Her curtains were
closed. The lights off.

Braudy pushed Tom towards the truck, opened the driver's
door, and he climbed in. The leather seat was cold. Braudy
closed the door and walked around the front of the truck. Tom

wondered how far he could run before Braudy would manage to fire a shot. Five metres. Ten. He could hide away in the shadows. Maybe the noise of gunshots would wake someone.

Braudy climbed in to the truck and pulled down the sock monkey charm from the rearview mirror. He threw it out of the window and lowered his gun to put on his seatbelt. Slowly, Tom reached for the handle to open the door, but stopped when he felt cold metal press against his temple.

'Hands on the wheel,' said Braudy. 'Ten to two.'

Tom looked straight ahead. He was handed the car keys.

'It's the one with the plastic fob. Shape of a cloud.'

Tom found the right key and put it in the ignition. He put on his seat belt.

'I want you to take the truck out quickly. If you hear a shot, keep driving. Understood?'

'Yeah.'

'You take us back to Bradford,' he said. 'Nice and steady. Understand?'

Tom started the engine and he switched on the headlights. The truck stalled. Tom started it again and the Bothy's lights came on. First the upstairs. Then the downstairs. He reversed the truck out into the road. The tyres slipped where it was still icy. Ken ran out into the front yard. He was dressed in silk pyjamas and held a gun in his right hand.

'Go, go, go!' shouted Braudy.

Tom hit the accelerator, and the truck bucked forward. There was a flash and then a bang. Something sparked to Tom's right. He heard another bang and the wing mirror shattered. Then there was a sharp noise behind him. He turned to see a crack in the back window.

'Look at the fucking road,' said Braudy.

Tom kept his foot down and took a corner quickly. He felt the back of the truck kick out as they hit some ice. He slowed down and gripped the wheel. In the distance, Tom could see the dark outline of the hills. A gap in the clouds, a faint glimmer of starlight.

Braudy looked back, and said, 'Keep it at twenty.'

Tom glanced down at the door handle again. He thought about jumping out. Maybe he would land on a patch of un-thawed snow. Some soft heather. He would suffer broken bones.

He heard the click of a safety, and saw the gun in the corner of his eye.

'Ten to two,' said Braudy. He pointed the gun at Tom's legs.

'You know Frank will come after you.'

'Way I see it, I'm saving everyone's neck.'

'Except mine.'

'You never know. Wayne might take pity on you.'

The truck skidded on a bend. The snow was still thick in places. Tom saw a sheep in the middle of the road. It trotted along, following the white lines. It stopped on a verge to chew the grass. Tom watched the sheep disappear in the rearview mirror. He took his foot off the accelerator for a moment. Braudy switched on the heaters. The skin on the tip of his nose had started to peel off in small flakes. He touched his infected ear with the blackened tips of his fingers.

'What did you do to your girlfriend, Tom? They can't want you dead because of a fucking car accident.'

'You don't know these people.'

'What was it? You beat her up? Cheat on her?'

'I never hurt her.'

'You can lie to yourself all you like.'

'You don't understand.'

'Save your breath, Tom. It's between you and them. Not my concern. I'll tell you that's one fucking thing Frank's taught me. Never mix business with emotion.'

'That's rich coming from you,' replied Tom.

'I'm surprised Frank didn't want to hand you over himself.'

'He's got his reasons.'

'Know what they are?'

'I think so.'

'You think so,' said Braudy. 'Right.'

'None of this will bring Tucker back, will it?'

'I need to start thinking about me now, Tom.'

'By getting me killed?'

'Well. Thought I might get some work out of it. Think I'll be rewarded for my initiative.'

'Initiative?'

'No-one else thought of doing this, did they?'

'Tucker did.'

Braudy pointed the gun at Tom's head. 'You keep quiet from now on. Understand?'

Tom looked ahead. They passed another stray sheep. It stood in a ditch near a collapsed wall. It munched on grass. Its fleece was marked with red dye.

Braudy reached over to turn down the heater. He was distracted. It was all Tom needed. He quickly struck out with his elbow and hit Braudy in his bad ear. He cried out. The gun went off. The bullet hit the back seat with a dull thud.

Braudy punched Tom in the kidneys. Two, three times. Tom reached up and tried to elbow Braudy away. He bit Braudy's hand and held him off. As he tried to control the truck, he caught a glimpse of something on the road ahead. Bright, white objects in the headlights. Sheep. Four or five of them. He hit the brakes but it was too late. Some of the sheep were caught under the wheels. Another was thrown over the bonnet and hit the windscreen. The truck glanced off the stone wall. There were sparks. A painful scrape of metal.

The truck collided with a telegraph pole and both men were thrown forward. The engine died. Steam rose up from the bonnet. Tom could hear the wind. The pained cries of wounded animals. In a daze, Tom looked over and saw Braudy slumped against the door. He gave him a push. He didn't move.

It took Tom a few tries to open the door. He got out and walked across a bloodied patch of snow. His hands shook and his chest ached. It was painful to breathe. He moved away to the side of the road and staggered past the injured sheep. The tarmac was slick with blood. One of the sheep was still alive. Twitching. Its eyes wild and fearful. Tom could not look at it. He clutched himself for warmth and stood by the stone wall. He vomited on to the cold grass. There was a noise from the truck. The passenger door squeaked open. Braudy stumbled out holding a torch. His face was bleeding and he stood there for a moment. Dazed and looking around. He saw Tom, raised his gun, and fired. A clump of dirt kicked up from the muddy embankment.

The second bang seemed louder. Tom jumped over the wall and landed in mud and snow. At the far end of the field there were beech trees all about ten or fifteen metres tall. Their naked branches were just about visible against the night sky. Snow had drifted up against the trunks. Tom ducked down. Braudy limped along the road towards him and shot the injured sheep in the head.

Tom moved along the wall until he reached a barbed wire fence. Tufts of wool wound around points on the strands, on the posts. Tom crouched in the shadows. His kidneys ached. A cut had opened above his left eye. A cold wind blew. He shivered.

Braudy clambered over the wall. He followed a faint path leading down to the trees. He called out Tom's name. His voice was hoarse. Strangely elated. Tom stayed hidden. He glanced up at the sky. The clouds were clearing. The slow reveal of thousands of stars. He moved his hand near the base of the wall and felt about for a rock or a branch. He found a rock the size of a honeydew melon. He crept forward. His feet crunched on the snow.

'Come out! We'll talk,' shouted Braudy.

Tom kept creeping along. Trying not to slip.

Braudy reached the trees and shouted out again, pleading this time. He shone his torch on a sheep capering away down the hill.

'Let's fucking talk. It's cold. Neither of us are going anywhere, Tom. The truck's busted.' He leaned on the trees, waiting for an answer.

Tom could see the top of Braudy's head was bloodied. His coat was torn at the back and the stuffing inside was visible. He held his infected ear and called out again.

Tom drew close and hurled the rock at Braudy. It hit his head and he fell to his knees, dropping the gun into the dirty snow. He held his hand up as if he had just remembered something important.

Tom darted in and picked up the gun. Braudy tried to

stand up but could not. He rested against a tree and looked at Tom. His eyes were glassy.

'Give me the keys, Braudy.'

'The keys?' His speech was slurred.

'The keys to the truck.'

'What happened to my head?'

'Braudy. Give me the keys,' said Tom.

Braudy shook his head, mystified. 'Keys,' he said, touching his infected ear. He looked upwards and closed his eyes. It did not take very long for him to die.

Tom picked up the torch and put on Braudy's coat and socks. Warm and moist. The boots were too small, but they would have to do. He checked the coat pockets and found the keys and headed back to the road. He could no longer feel his toes. He checked the cut over his left eye. It had stopped bleeding.

The truck's headlights were still on but he could smell petrol and saw something leaking from the bottom of the truck. Even if the engine worked, there wouldn't be enough fuel to get him far. He stopped by a ditch and had a piss. It hurt.

He headed back to the Bothy, trying to ignore the blisters on his feet. He counted as he walked. When he got to fifty, he stopped and gave himself a minute to rest. Then he started again, sticking to the parts of the road where the snow had melted. After half a mile he passed some sheep gathered near a broken fence. He guessed they were from the same flock as the others he had hit in the truck.

He carried on, but got no sense he was getting any closer to the Bothy. It was still only a small, bright light on a hill. He caught sight of rabbits in the fields, eyes turned silver from the torchlight. Some turned and ran. Others merely watched him. He kept going and stopped counting. Resting only worsened the pain in his feet.

It took him two hours to reach the Bothy. The lights were on. As he drew closer, he could see white smoke from the chimney. He caught the whiff of diesel and sewage. The thought of a warm fire spurred him on.

He crossed the yard and saw the sock monkey charm lying in a small mound of snow. He saw movement through the window. He entered the lobby and went through to the bar. The warmth of the room made his skin tingle. Ken sat near the window, sorting through bullets. He had a gun by his side. Cora sat nearby, holding a bag of ice over her right eye. She smoked a cigarette and did not look at Tom.

He tried to smile. 'I'm back.'

Ken lifted his gun. 'Put your fucking hands up.'

CHAPTER TWENTY-THREE

T OM WANTED TO take off the boots to see what state
his feet were in. The pain was bad and getting worse.
Cora got out of her seat. She lifted the icepack. Her bruised
eye was bloodshot. She stared at him for a moment and then
threw another log on the fire and watched it burn. The fireguard had been folded up and put to one side.

'Can I sit?' asked Tom.

Ken directed Tom into the middle of the room and stood
behind him. He patted him down and reached into his jacket
pocket and pulled out the car keys. He reached into the other
pocket and took out the gun and wiped the lint off it. He
sniffed the muzzle. 'You shoot him?'

'No.'

'Is he dead?'

'Yes.'

'And the truck?'

'Smashed up,' said Tom. 'We hit some sheep.'

'How bad?'

'The sheep are dead.'

'I mean the truck.'

'I don't know. Bad.' He glanced at Cora. She did not look
at him.

Ken pushed him out of the bar into the office. The blisters
on his feet were stinging. He felt blood squelch in his boots.
The tips of his fingers were dark red and numb. Ken shoved

him forward down the corridor and unlocked the metal door. He switched on the lights and pushed Tom into the room.

The door slammed shut and the lock turned. The clean white walls made the room seem vast. The tap in the corner of the room dripped. A small trickle of water dribbled into the rusty drain. He limped over to the trestle table pushed up against the back wall. On it, there was a paint brush set, still in its plastic packaging. A roll of paper towels. Tom took off Braudy's jacket and pulled off his boots. He peeled off the bloody socks and hobbled over to the tap in the corner. He washed his feet under cold water and tried to remove the grit and dirt from his grazed hands. Then he ripped off a length of paper towel and tried to clean the wounds. He lifted his jumper and T-shirt and inspected the bruises on his body. The shadows in the room shifted. The single bare lightbulb swung gently as someone moved about upstairs. There were a few pieces of stray duct tape hanging from the ceiling and the bright white walls. He put Braudy's coat over his shoulders and started to cry.

There were voices outside the room. Low and indistinct. The door opened. Tom wiped his eyes. Frank walked in. He was wearing combat trousers, a denim shirt, moccasins. His eyes were dull and tired. Ken brought in two plastic chairs, which he put in the centre of the room. Frank sat down and stretched out his legs. Tom hobbled over to him and took a seat.

Frank picked up the boots. 'Braudy bought these last year. In Worksop. And that coat. Was never sure about the colour.' He turned the coat over and looked at the blood on the collar.

'Ken,' said Frank. 'Get some bandages will you?'

'Where are they?'

'The toilet.'

'Need anything else?'

'Just the bandages.'

Ken left the room and Frank stared at Tom. They sat in silence. A draught blew through the cracks in the wall. Ken came back in with a green first aid box. He set the box down on the table, folded his arms, and put a strip of gum in his mouth.

'You've got a bloody nerve coming back here, Tom,' said Frank.

'I didn't want to leave. Braudy took me.'

Frank reached forward and grabbed Tom's foot. He squeezed. Tom tried hard not to cry out. 'There's another reason you came back. Isn't there?'

He squeezed Tom's foot harder. Blood oozed from the cuts and dripped on the concrete floor.

'You came back for Cora. Didn't you?'

'No.'

'Why had she packed her bags?'

'I don't know.'

Frank squeezed again. 'You two. Planning to run. That it, Tom?'

'No.'

'Say it louder. Like you mean it.'

'No!'

Frank let go of the foot and went over to the tap in the corner of the room. He washed the blood from his hands. Ken handed him a paper towel.

'Bad enough that you crashed the fucking truck,' said Frank.

'What are we going to do with him?'

Frank dried his hands and said, 'Tom won't mind staying here for a day or two. Go and get him a sleeping bag.'

'What about your plan?' asked Tom.

'Which plan?'

'That if Wayne saw me, he'd think that Galloway couldn't have made it up here.'

'Ken reckons it's better if you stay out of sight. After all that's happened.'

Tom moved to stand up. Ken pushed him back down in his seat.

'I need to go for a piss,' said Tom.

'Now?'

Tom touched his bruised kidneys and nodded. Ken pointed a gun at the back of his head.

'Take it easy with him, Ken.'

Tom was guided out of the room. Grit from the dirty floor got into his cuts and he left a trail of bloody footsteps. He walked slowly down the corridor and went into the toilet. The pull switch had been fixed. As he pissed, he gasped in pain. His urine was a light shade of pink. He finished and stepped out of the bathroom. He looked towards the open metal door. A knife of light cut into the dark corridor.

Frank was standing in the centre of the safe room, staring into space, pinching his bottom lip between thumb and forefinger. Ken took the two chairs outside. Tom went over to the trestle table and Frank left the room.

The locks clicked. The lights flickered. Tom opened up the first aid box. There were antiseptic wipes. White Hello Kitty plasters. An old tube of Deep Heat. He put Braudy's jacket on the floor and sat down on it. He cleaned his wounds and his bruised face with the wipes. He touched the welts, the inflamed skin. Then, he applied the plasters to the cuts on his heels and toes. Exhausted, he put his head against the wall and closed his eyes.

He woke up to the jangle of keys, the click of the lock. Tom did not stand. He looked at his feet. The plasters were already stained red. The metal door opened. Ken came in holding a blue inflatable mattress, a red foot pump, a sleeping bag, and a pillow. He threw the bedding on the ground, and left the room. Frank came in with two cups of coffee. He handed Tom a cup and went to sit on a table.

'Should warm you up a bit,' he said.

'I thought we'd run out of coffee.'

'Cora had some in her room. Told me she was saving it for a special occasion.'

'Oh.'

Frank got up and looked closely at Tom.

'Looks like you've got chillblains,' he said. 'On your nose.'

Tom held up his hands. His fingers were blue.

'Hot drink will help. I can get you some painkillers if you like.'

Tom tried the coffee. It tasted different from the other stuff. Smoother.

Frank drew breath in through his teeth. 'After you left with Braudy, we found other stuff in Cora's room. A brown envelope stuffed with fifties.'

Tom put his coffee down.

'Funny. It was the money what did it for me. Made me lose my temper a bit.' He paused. 'It was more of a slap than anything else.'

'Frank. Jesus.'

226

'I don't know what to believe any more. Now Braudy's gone. Seems like one less certainty.'

'I had to kill him, Frank.' Tom swirled around the coffee grounds in the bottom of his cup. 'You understand that, don't you?'

'Had to protect yourself. I know.'

Frank finished his coffee and took both their cups to the tap in the corner of the room and rinsed them out. The brown water trickled down into the grating.

Frank left. Tom heard the locks turn. The lights remained on. He inflated the mattress with the red foot pump. He climbed into the sleeping bag and lay down. There was a slow puncture. It hissed softly. He covered his face with the pillow and fell asleep.

CHAPTER TWENTY-FOUR

TOM HEARD VOICES outside. Laughter. He put his ear against the cold metal door. There was a gentle popping sound. Like Champagne corks or distant fireworks. He backed away and heard two loud bangs. The locks clicked and the door opened. A man stood there, holding a Glock pistol and a bunch of keys with a key fob attached. The man was wearing a black boiler suit, neatly pressed. Hair dark. Eyes grey. It was Nixon. One of Wayne's men. He stepped into the room and looked at the white walls and ceilings.

'It's Tom, isn't it?' asked Nixon.

'Yeah.'

'Thought they'd give you a nicer room than this.' He kicked at the partially deflated lilo. 'Get your kecks on. Boss wants to meet you.'

Tom sat down and got dressed. The cuts on his feet had started to bleed again.

'Got any shoes?'

'No.'

Tom was ushered out of the room. He limped down the corridor, through to the kitchen. Only one of the strip lights was on.

Wayne sat at the table in the middle of the room. He was different from how Tom remembered him. Fatter, with bad skin. He was dressed in a sky-blue suit, gold-shaded shirt and black tie. The blazer was tight around the chest, the trouser legs riding up, revealing the tops of his green silk socks. He was reading one of the old menus. Chuckling. In front of him he had three plastic bags. Cartons of fried chicken. Sausages and battered fish wrapped in white paper. A jar of Frank's pickled eggs. Cans of soft drinks. Cola, lemonade. Dandelion and Burdock.

Wayne stood up and came over to Tom. The smell of the unwashed polyester suit was partially masked by sweet-smelling aftershave. Egg on his breath. He held Tom's chin and examined his blistered and bruised skin. Wayne turned to Nixon and said, 'Is there any ice? For Tom's bruises?'

Nixon pulled out a bag of peas from the freezer compartment. He wrapped it in a tea towel and handed it to Tom. He held it over his bruised cheek and cut eye.

'Don't look after you, do they, mate?' He looked down at Tom's bleeding feet. 'Why don't you come in and take a load off? Have something to eat.'

Tom pulled a stool up to the table and sat down.

Wayne sat opposite him and said, 'Have a look in the fridge, Nixon.'

Nixon opened the fridge and looked surprised when he saw Ken's socks neatly piled up near the salad crisper. He picked out the carton of yoghurt.

'This went out of date last year,' said Nixon.

'Ken didn't want to throw it away,' replied Tom.

'Mad cunt.'

'Why don't you put that down,' said Wayne, 'and give Tom a nice pair of socks that won't hurt his feet.'

Nixon picked out some lime-coloured socks. Tom put them on and savoured the coolness of the fabric. He looked at the food on the table again and saw the glossy flesh of a saveloy sausage poke through white paper. Something had been drawn on the paper with biro. A 'V'.

'You must be starving,' said Wayne, eating a chip.

'You didn't bring this for me.'

'This is for everyone. Get stuck in. Have some chips at least.'

Tom looked at the bags of food. He could smell vinegar. Gravy. Deep-fat frying. His stomach made a noise. He paused and then said quietly, 'Can I have some fish?'

'Go ahead.'

Tom unwrapped the fish carefully. His fingers were still numb and he clumsily picked up a blue plastic fork. He scraped away at the pieces of batter stuck to the greasy paper.

Wayne took off his blazer. He wore a leather shoulder holster which carried a snub-nosed pistol with a walnut grip. He reached into the jar, plucked out an egg, and chewed it slowly, noisily.

'I'm going to miss these,' he said. 'You a fan?'

'Never tried one.' Tom broke off another piece of batter and ate it. He watched Nixon run his hand over the kitchen wall and brush flaking plaster from his fingers. 'You got a damp problem up here?' he asked.

'It's an old house,' said Tom.

'Should be condemned,' replied Nixon.

Wayne ate the other half of the egg. He licked the vinegar off his fingers. 'Frank ever tell you about Mandy?'

'Only a little.'

'Nice woman. Too much fun for a miserable bastard like Frank,' said Wayne, taking out a cigarette and Frank's gold Dupont lighter.

'Cracking lass,' said Nixon.

'Why did she leave?' asked Tom.

'The first time was because Frank drowned her cat in the septic tank.'

'And the second time?'

'Frank always told us she went to back to Toxteth,' he said, lighting his cigarette. 'I have family out there. They never fucking saw her.'

'They told me Leeds,' said Tom.

'Or she went to Blackpool. That was the other story they told.'

'Or she went to fucking Timbuktu,' said Nixon.

'We've been fed the same shit, Tom. Don't you worry,' said Wayne. 'Frank told me Tucker and Braudy had left too. Recently. How did he put it, Nixon?'

'Said they both left under a bit of a cloud.'

'You remember a guy called Galloway?' asked Wayne. 'He was here when we last met. Me, Galloway, Nixon. Sachin.'

'I remember,' said Tom.

'Well, Sachin's up here today. And someone who used to work for Frank.'

'That gave him a bit of a surprise,' said Nixon.

'They're both in the other room. Looking after Ken, Frank, and Cora.'

'No Galloway, then?'

Wayne looked over at Nixon and smirked. 'Good. Isn't he?'

'Class,' replied Nixon, reaching into one of the bags. He took out a large fishcake and broke it in two. The greyish flesh was flaky.

'You can drop the act, Tom. Galloway came up here about a week ago.'

'Before or after the snow?'

Wayne sighed and said, 'Galloway texted me up here. Told me he was five miles away. Said it was snowing. That was the last I heard from him.'

Tom pushed his food about with the plastic fork. He didn't look up. Wayne shifted in his chair and his suit crackled. He finished his cigarette and asked, 'You know why he came up here, don't you?'

Tom tapped the top of a can of lemonade and opened it. He took a sip and felt the bubbles on his tongue.

'Did you ever speak to Frank about the price on your head?' asked Wayne.

'Yeah.'

'Normally, lots of these contracts are in the low thousands. But this one? Wow.'

'You saying I should be flattered?'

Wayne leaned forward and lowered his voice. 'I really have nothing against you, Tom. Nothing at all. I've done some work for the people who want you. That prick Conway.'

'Like what?'

'Whatever a prick like Conway needs. He pays well. Lets us get on with it. That's probably the best you can say about the fucker though. What was that last meeting like, Nixon?'

'The stupid tit just ate chocolates and told us how much he was worth.'

'I wish we didn't have to deal with him. I'm sure you had your fill of his nonsense.'

'I had Christmas dinner with them once.'

'And how was that?'

'How you'd expect.'

'Bet the crackers were good,' said Nixon.

'Still the same shit jokes inside?'

'Yeah.'

Wayne ate a chip and said, 'They're offering a lot of money for you. We know it. You know it. Frank knows it too.'

'What's your point?'

Wayne pursed his lips and tried to find the right words. 'You've not thought much about this. Have you?'

'About what?'

'Why Frank didn't want to hand you in himself.'

'He said he wouldn't.'

'Yet he locks you away in that room?'

'Like fucking Rapunzel,' said Nixon.

Tom looked at the chip paper. The yellow stains of grease.

'Maybe when he first took you on,' said Wayne, 'he thought he was helping a fugitive. Protecting someone from the law, maybe. Or injustice. Or he saw something of himself in you. Some sentimental shit like that. But when he found out about the price on your head, I bet he had a little tingle at the back of his mind. Like what it might be like to have all that money. What he could do with it.'

'He might have done.'

'But he's a good man so wouldn't act on it? That what you think?'

'It's what he said.'

Wayne laughed and shook his head. 'You seem like a sweet boy, Tom.'

Nixon looked in the cupboard under the sink. He took out a black bin liner and started to fill it with the greasy paper and cartons. Wayne burped and waved away the smell. He put on his blazer. 'You finished eating?'

'Yeah,' said Tom.

He sat back and turned to Nixon. 'What do you think we should do with Ken and Frank? Take them back to Leeds?'

'May as well do it here.'

'Sure?'

Nixon nodded. He threw drinks cans and wrappers into the black bag.

'What happens to Cora?' asked Tom.

Wayne rose to his feet and said, 'Hard to keep women like that quiet.'

There was a sound from another part of the building. Something hard and metallic. Then the lights in the corridor went out. Wayne glanced over Tom's shoulder and took the pistol out from his holster.

'Go and take a look, Nixon.'

Nixon stopped tidying the rubbish and went to the door. He tried the lights in the corridor. They weren't working. He peered into the murk and raised his pistol. There was a flash. A loud bang. A volley of buckshot hit Nixon and blasted him backwards against the side of a refrigerator.

Tom flattened himself on the floor and covered his ears. Wayne hid behind one of the kitchen units. Nixon tried to get to his feet and fired two shots into the darkness. There was another loud bang. Thick, dark blood spurted from Nixon's chest and throat. He dropped to his knees and fell against the crumbling plaster wall. Dust and gun smoke filled the room.

Ken moved out from the dark corridor. Calmly reloading a shotgun. Rattling the cartridges close to his ear before pushing them into the chamber. His face was bruised. He had a wound in his side, and his white shirt was red and wet.

Tom stayed on the floor, covering his head with his hands. Wayne's face was expressionless.

Ken limped into the kitchen and kicked Nixon's gun away across the linoleum. He looked at Tom. Without anger or fear.

'Let's talk about this, Ken,' said Wayne.

Ken smiled, and calmly lifted the shotgun.

'Ken. Let's talk.'

Wayne moved from behind the kitchen unit, raised his gun, and took a shot. There was a fizz from the gun. And nothing else. Wayne squeezed the trigger again. There was a delay. A fizz, and then a bang. The bullet punched a hole in the wall by the cupboards.

Ken smiled and fired the shotgun. Buckshot hit Wayne in the chest, throwing him backwards against the wall. Blood splattered on the floor. The oven and the fridge. Wayne slid to the ground, still breathing. His shirt darkened with blood.

Ken marched over to him, picked up the pistol, and looked at it with dull eyes.

Tom got up off the floor with his hands up. 'Please. Ken. Don't shoot.'

'Shut up.' He touched his wounded side and took two more cartridges from his pocket. He listened to them and loaded them into the shotgun.

Tom left Ken sitting in the kitchen, and limped down the corridor, squinting in the darkness.

He went through to the office. There were no sounds. No voices. He entered the bar. There was a smell of sweat and flesh. He stepped over two bodies in the middle of the room. The men wore shirts and ties. One of them had his trousers around his ankles. Both had their navy-coloured blazers torn from gunshots. The carpet was sodden with blood and brains. Furniture was smashed. Four glasses were lined up on the bar. They were filled with dark frothy bitter.

Frank was standing behind the bar. He was dressed in a dark suit. The shirt open at the collar, the tie loose around his neck. His face was badly bruised. Eyes puffy. Lips still bloody. He smoked a cigarette and held a Smith and Wesson by his side.

'Where's Ken?' asked Frank.

'He's been shot.'

'Dead?'

'No.'

Cora was sitting in the corner. Her skirt and jumper were ripped. Her face was pale but her eyes remained steady. She was drinking water from a tall glass. Her hands shook.

Tom stepped around an upturned table.

Frank poured himself a drink. 'Want one? Just to settle the nerves?'

'A brandy.'

Frank filled a glass and passed it to Tom.

'Drink it down in one,' said Frank.

Tom nodded, and glanced over at Cora. She did not look at him.

'You won't get an answer from her.'

'Should we get a blanket or something? To keep her warm.'

'In a minute. Come on. Drink up.'

Tom drank his brandy. He looked outside. A large green car was parked in the yard. Cora put her glass of water down on the floor. She brushed at her torn clothes and sighed.

Frank stretched and put the Smith and Wesson in the waistband of his trousers.

Ken walked into the room holding his injured side. He sat down on the bench. His breathing was shallow. He took out Wayne's snub-nosed pistol and dried the grip on his shirt.

Then he reached into his pocket, took out some bullets, and loaded them into the magazine.

Frank handed him a whisky and held up Wayne's gun to the light. He weighed it in his hand.

'This must be worth a bit,' he said.

'Custom made. Shit ammo.'

Frank gave the gun back to Ken.

'Where are you hit?'

Ken lifted his shirt. Blood oozed from a wound in his abdomen. Frank drew breath in through his teeth. He took a damp black bar towel and pressed it against Ken's wound.

'Hold that there.'

'I know what to do,' replied Ken. His breath was ragged. His skin pale. He sipped his whisky and lay down on the bench.

'Me and Tom are going to clear up a little,' said Frank. 'Then we'll come back and sort all this out.'

Ken nodded and exhaled.

Frank knelt in front of Cora. He touched the bruises on her face. The fresh ones and the ones he'd caused. She brushed his hand away. He smiled sadly and cast his eyes about the wrecked room before gesturing for Tom to follow him. They walked through the office, past the workbenches.

'Look in that cupboard, Tom.'

'Here?'

'Yeah. Should be some cellophane packets.'

Tom opened the cupboard. He reached in, and pulled out a shower curtain, still in its plastic wrapping.

'Get two,' he said.

The corridor was dark. The bulbs loosened, or the wires cut. The kitchen was still smoky. It smelled of blood and shit. Frank whistled at the scene, half-smiling. He looked at Nixon slumped against the wall. Wayne had managed to crawl halfway across the room, smearing the linoleum with blood.

Frank searched Wayne's blazer, and pulled out car keys. A wallet. He found the Dupont lighter and put it in his pocket. He leaned close to Wayne and said, 'Can you hear me, you piece of shit?'

There was a groan.

Frank slapped Wayne's face.

Wayne blinked and tried to lift his head. Blood bubbled on his lips. He tried to speak. Frank grinned and looked back at Tom.

'Told you I'd get rid of the bastard for you.'

Tom stepped back towards one of the fridges. His fingers brushed against the holes caused by the buckshot. His socks were sticky with blood.

Wayne placed his fingers on Frank's cheek and his eyes widened. A smile formed on his lips. He patted Frank on the cheek. Frank pushed his hand away and stood up.

'I won, you fucking twat. Me.'

He stamped on Wayne's head. Over and over again. Tom turned away.

Frank wiped his boots on Wayne's back. He went to the sink and splashed his face with cold water. Then he opened the cellophane packets and laid out the shower curtains next to the two bodies. The curtains were patterned with anchors, starfish.

'What happens after this?' asked Tom.

'Thought we could eat some of that food.' He had a look in the plastic bags. 'Chinese. Curry. Not bad.'

'I mean with your work. With Wayne gone.'

'Just happy this is over. You should be happy too, Tom. Now you're safe.'

'I don't think I am safe,' said Tom.

Frank wiped at his mouth with his thumb, and lifted Wayne by the ankles, touching the green silk socks. With Tom's help, he rolled him on to the shower curtain so he lay face up. They did the same with Nixon. Tom looked at the body at his feet. Half-wrapped in the plastic sheeting. Staring eyes. Mouth gaping.

'We'll take them out to Wayne's car,' said Frank.

Tom picked up the end of the shower curtain, hooking his fingers through the eyelets. He pulled. The plastic curtain hissed as it passed over the linoleum. When he entered the corridor it sounded like he was dragging something across sandpaper.

Frank wasn't far behind, muttering to himself. Tom continued to pull Nixon along. Some of the blood leaked through a tear in the shower curtain, leaving behind a red streak. He stopped. His feet were sore. His muscles ached.

'What did Wayne say to you?' asked Frank.

'Told me I wasn't safe.'

'Yeah. From him. And now he's dead—'

'You're going to hand me over to the Conways, aren't you? For the money.'

Frank rubbed his chin and looked down at Wayne's corpse.

'Is that what you think?' he asked.

'I know it's true, Frank.'

He smiled sadly and took out his gun. Tom raised his hands.

'No need for that, Tom. Just walk.'

They walked through to the bar. It was as they had left

it. Ken was still lying on the bench. The black bar towel had fallen to the floor. His bullet wound no longer seeped. Cora stepped out from behind the bar. She was holding Wayne's gun.

'What happened to Ken?' asked Frank.

'He stopped breathing five minutes ago,' she replied.

'And you did nothing to help him?'

'Give me Wayne's car keys,' said Cora.

Frank smiled and shook his head. He quickly grabbed Tom. He took his Smith and Wesson and held it to Tom's head.

She steadied the gun and stared down the sights.

Frank pushed the gun up against Tom's cheek. Tom's nose. He held him tight. He held his arm around his throat. 'You shoot, his brains will end up on the specials board.'

'Give me the fucking keys.'

Frank grinned and moved forward. He pressed the pistol under Tom's chin. 'You know about our friend Tom here?'

'What about him?'

'We hand him in alive, we get quarter of a million quid, Cora. Quarter of a million quid.'

'Shut up,' she said.

'Put that gun down and I'll split it with you. Sixty-forty.'

'Shut up.'

'Sixty-forty. Your favour.'

She didn't answer but gripped the gun tight.

'Doing the arithmetic, Cora?' He grinned. 'Raise me to seventy-thirty if you like.'

She clenched her jaw and narrowed her eyes.

'Think about it. Think about how far you could go with that money. A new fucking life. Sunshine. The beach.'

Tom saw something change in her expression.

'It's more than enough money, Cora. You'll be free from me. And you can buy as many fucking shoes as you like.'

Cora shook her head. Smiled. 'That's what you think I'd spend the money on?'

'Do we have a deal?' he asked.

'No, we don't have a fucking deal. Give me the keys. To the car.'

'That gun you have. Know anything about it? The ammo Wayne used?'

Her arms shook and she changed her stance, moving backwards slightly.

'That cunt Wayne never had a man as good as Ken,' said Frank. 'Never tested his fucking bullets.'

'Shut up.'

'Fifty-fifty that gun won't go off.'

'Fuck off, Frank,' she said, squeezing the trigger. There was a load bang. Tom felt the bullet graze his right ear. It hit Frank on the nose and passed through the back of his head. Thud. Tom looked back and saw Frank fall to his knees. She shot him again and he fell backwards. His brains leaked out on to the carpet.

She put the gun down. There was a smell of gun smoke. Tom was covered in Frank's blood. He touched his right ear. It burned but there was no blood. He looked over at Frank. He thought he saw movement. A twitch of a finger. The flicker of an eyelid. Cora walked over and pushed at the corpse with her foot. She lit a cigarette and leaned against the bar. He sat next to her. There was a thickness in the air. The bodies on the floor had started to stink. The blood on the carpet was hardening. His hands shook. Cora brought him a glass of whisky and then went behind the bar. She opened the cash register.

It was empty except for the two ten pound notes Tom had handed to Ken on the first night. The only other thing in the cash register was a bag of five pence pieces and a small wooden carving in the shape of a penis. She gave Tom the two tenners and went over to Frank's corpse. She searched him and found Wayne's car keys. She walked around the bodies of Wayne's men. She reached up and moved one of the horse brasses.

'Frank took my money,' she said.

'Where?'

'His room.'

'I'll wait.'

'Help me look.'

Tom followed her out to the office. She tried the lights and walked up the stairs. He was relieved to get away from the smell in the bar. They crossed the landing. Cora opened Frank's bedroom door. The windows were bricked up, the walls painted marigold. A white wardrobe sat in the corner. Tom looked up and saw an oval mirror mounted on the ceiling above the bed. It reflected a lozenge of light on to the wall opposite. Four pairs of shoes were carefully lined up near the single bed. The white duvet was straightened out and the pillows still bore the impression of Frank's head. A single banker's lamp sat on a desk. Cora opened the drawers and pulled out files and pieces of paper. She opened the wardrobe in the corner and took out Frank's clothes. Beneath ironed shirts she found a large jiffy bag. It was filled with cash. Bundles of fifties.

'Where did you get it from?'

'Frank wanted me to buy the same sort of underwear Mandy used to wear. Never bothered. Hid it instead.'

'Is the money all there?'

She nodded and sat down on the bed. Tom sat next to her and looked at the wall. He put his hands down on the sheet and left a bloody stain. She touched her torn clothes. There were spots of blood on it. 'Did you want to do it?' he asked.

'Do what?'

'Did you want to hand me over and split the money with Frank?'

'It's a lot of money.'

'I wouldn't have blamed you.'

'That's because you still want to punish yourself. For her.'

Tom's hand touched Cora's. She held it and squeezed gently. They lay back on the bed and both looked up at the ceiling. Weariness overcame him and he fell asleep.

When he woke up he was alone. He got up and went to the bathroom and washed his hands and face until the water ran clear. He dried his hands on a soft mauve towel. His bedroom still smelled of sweat. He saw his pair of Oxfords on the bed and sat down. There was a small pile of fifty pound notes under his pillow. He pushed the money aside and wondered when Cora had left. He looked out at the far blue hills. The distant fields. The light changed until it was no longer clear, no longer bright.

ACKNOWLEDGEMENTS

I WOULD LIKE to thank my family and friends for their support, and Joe Stretch and my editor Nicholas Royle for their amazing help and advice. Extra special thanks to Kirstie McCrum for putting up with my nonsense for all these years.

This book has been typeset by
SALT PUBLISHING LIMITED
using Neacademia, a font designed by Sergei Egorov
for the Rosetta Type Foundry in the Czech Republic. It
is manufactured using Holmen Book Cream 70gsm,
a Forest Stewardship Council™ certified paper from the
Hallsta Paper Mill in Sweden. It was printed and bound
by Clays Limited in Bungay, Suffolk, Great Britain.

CROMER
GREAT BRITAIN
MMXIX